# LIFE EVERLASTING

# LIFE EVERLASTING

## Or, The Delights awaiting the Faithful Soul in Paradise ❧ ❧ ❧

*By the Right Rev.* JOHN S. VAUGHAN,
BISHOP OF SEBASTOPOLIS, *Author of "Life after Death," etc., etc.*

'Venit hora, in qua omnes, qui in monumentis sunt, audient vocem Filii Dei.'—JOHN v. 28.

'Merces sanctorum : 1, tam *magna* est, quod non potest mensurari,
2, tam *copiosa*, quod non potest finiri.
3, tam *pretiosa*, quod non potest aestimari.'
ST. AMBROSE.

P. J. KENEDY & SONS
4 BARCLAY STREET, NEW YORK
1922

NIHIL OBSTAT:

F. THOMAS BERGH, O.S.B.,

*Censor Deputatus.*

IMPRIMATUR:

EDM. CAN. SURMONT,

*Vicarius Generalis.*

✠ WESTMONASTERII,

*Die* 6 *Novembris*, 1922.

PRINTED IN ENGLAND

## AUTHOR'S PREFACE

IN spite of the magnificent gift of reason with which man has been endowed, what a strangely inconsistent creature he is! This inconsistency is so great as to be patent to every observer, while the evidences of it are even more striking in the supernatural order than in the natural. Take a few simple examples. Thus, every Catholic admits that sin is by far the greatest of all possible calamities, yet many *act* as though it were the very least! Or, to take another instance, all candidly acknowledge that Divine grace is the most priceless of treasures, and that one additional degree of actual grace surpasses in intrinsic value all the accumulated treasures of the entire material universe. Yet, in practice, many will make no effort to increase their store, or even to safeguard the little they already possess. But I have dwelt upon these points before.* On this

* In the pages of *The Irish Ecclesiastical Record.*

occasion I propose referring to another glaring inconsistency, and that is, to the ordinary Catholic's attitude towards the happiness which God has solemnly promised to those who are willing to serve Him loyally during the few years of the present life—*i.e.*, the happiness of Heaven.

Let us start by considering that man has been adapted and indeed created for happiness. He can no more help seeking it than he can help breathing. From his first entry into this 'valley of tears' till he closes his eyes in the last sleep of death, he is always seeking after it. Even the poor, misguided wretch who hangs himself, or who throws himself under a passing train, is no exception to the universal rule. He destroys himself to avoid a painful crisis which he dare not face, and commits suicide because he imagines that, owing to his present trials and misfortunes, he will be happier dead than alive. Thus, all men, without exception, pursue happiness, though not all pursue it where it may truly be found.

Now the question arises: If all men are attracted even by such an inadequate happiness as this world can afford, how comes it that the infinitely greater happiness offered by God awakes so little enthusiasm and arouses such ineffectual desires? Let us state the case as simply as possible. Thus: A Catholic is taught, and sincerely believes, that there is awaiting him beyond the grave, provided he leads an ordinary good life, a happiness incomparably intenser and inconceivably greater than any happiness the world can ever offer him, even though he were the luckiest and the most favoured of men. He knows full well that it is a happiness, not merely immeasurably more intense and more satisfying and joy-yielding than any happiness he can ever look forward to in this world, but also a pure, unadulterated, unclouded happiness, without any admixture of sorrow, care, or anxiety to mar its perfection, and—what is perhaps of still greater importance—a happiness absolutely secure and absolutely permanent. Furthermore, he is assured, and readily accepts the statement, that any soul, *with the experience of both states before him*, would undoubtedly deem it a higher privilege and a far more desirable favour to gaze on the unveiled Face of God for the space of one minute than to swim in an ocean of earthly delights for a thousand years.

The ordinary conscientious Catholic may indeed wonder at the doctrine, as expressed by learned theologians and inspired saints, who dilate upon the ecstatic joys of the Beatific Vision, but he will hardly question its substantial truth. Thus he does not suspect St. John of the Cross of exaggeration when he writes:

'Two visions are fatal to man, because he cannot bear them. One, that of the basilisk, at the sight of which men are said to die at once. The other is the vision of God; but there is a great difference between them. The former kills by poison, the other with infinite bliss and glory. It is therefore nothing strange for the soul to desire to die by beholding the beauty of God, in order to enjoy Him for ever. . . .

'If [he goes on to say] the soul had but *one single glimpse* of the grandeur and beauty of God, it would not only desire to die once, in order to behold Him, but would endure joyfully a *thousand most bitter deaths to behold Him, even for a moment,* and having seen Him once, would suffer as many deaths again to see Him for another moment.'*

Think, then, what the delight must be of seeing and enjoying Him, in all His splendour and magnificence, for an endless eternity!

Though Archbishop Kirby does not speak with the authority of St. John, yet he faithfully interprets the teaching of the Church when he writes:

'God's goodness, beauty, and amiability are immense. They are calculated to ravish the heart of every creature to such a degree as to render it *incomparably* better to behold Him FOR A SINGLE INSTANT THAN TO ENJOY FOR ALL ETERNITY ALL THE DELIGHTS OF THE UNIVERSE.'†

The same thought occurs in another passage on p. 94—viz.:

'So great is the amiability, and so great the perfections of God, that the damned would gladly suffer all their torments *a thousand times over,* could they but look, EVEN FOR A MOMENT, on that divine and

* 'Works,' vol. ii., p. 57. † 'Meditations,' p. 40.

heavenly countenance which the angels themselves desire to behold.'

Though there is no need of multiplying authorities, we will add just one more, who is a member of the Society of Jesus. After speaking of the happiness of an Eternity with God, Father Jn. Nieremberg, S.J., continues:

'But why do I insist upon eternity? Even though this glory were not eternal, but only momentary, yet it is a good so boundlessly great, that *an eternity of suffering cannot be deemed too much to purchase it, though only for a moment*, granting that, in that moment, we behold God intuitively.'*

Of course, man's reason itself will convince him that happiness must be greater or less according to the nature of the source from which it springs, and that consequently a happiness which is derived from the possession of a finite good can never approach in intensity, nor be compared in any way with a happiness which is derived from the possession of an infinite good. Yet it is evident that all earthly happiness is derived from finite objects. Men profess to find it in the possession

* 'Temporal and Eternal,' p. 372.

of bodily health, earthly pleasures, money, influence, authority, and in eating, drinking and carousing, as well as in music, dancing, display, sensual delights, and a host of other purely finite and created goods; whereas heavenly happiness is derived essentially from that which is uncreated, eternal, and infinite—namely, from God. 'I am thy reward, exceeding great' (Gen. xv. 1).

Strong as this argument is, its force becomes very much intensified when we begin to realize the intimate closeness of the mysterious union which takes place between God, the infinitely beautiful, and the glorified soul in Heaven. A vast number even of Catholics fall immeasurably short of the truth in their conception of the Beatific Vision.

Many picture Heaven to themselves as a kind of glorified theatre in which the Blessed sit around, in endless rows, tier above tier, gazing at the infinite beauty of God from a respectful distance. Yet, what could be more unlike the glorious reality? Père Lejeune's words are much to the point. After speaking of the wrong notions, he observes:

'His love demands much greater intimacy than that. He will unite Himself to us in the closest unity. He will be as the very air that we breathe; as the very torrent of delights with which we shall be inebriated, the life of our life, and our impassioned Lover. He will kiss us with the kisses of His mouth, and will receive the same from us. In short, He will not be satisfied until He, as it were, unites Himself with the loving soul, and until both melt together into one. . . . Heaven is not the mere sight of God, it is the being absorbed into God (*fusion avec Dieu*) by love and happiness.'*

It must be clearly borne in mind that:

'The vision of God by the Blessed in Heaven is not mere vision, but union; they see God as He is in Himself, not from a distance, as sensible objects are seen, nor by a discursive intellectual process as intelligible ideas are perceived, but, so to speak, from within. They are not, it is needless to say, pantheistically merged into God, but united to Him, by His supernatural action, so that the consciousness of the Divine

* Lejeune, 'Avant et Après la Communion,' p. 323.

Presence in the soul is akin to, and in some sense bound up with, its consciousness of itself. Therefore, as our self-consciousness is intellectual and yet immediate, so also the beatific vision of God is both immediate and intellectual. Hence it is not surprising that "St. Teresa could not distinguish between herself and God while in a state of rapture," and St. John of the Cross says that "the soul seems to be God rather than itself, and indeed is God by participation." '*

The ordinary devout Catholic, whose ideas of the next world are largely dependent upon his experiences in this, is apt to look upon God as a great King ruling His subjects, in His Kingdom of Heaven, with infinite benignity, and wisdom, and love indeed, but with even a greater aloofness, dignity, and reserve than characterize even the mightiest sovereigns here below. As an ordinary well-conducted subject in an earthly court might expect to receive a few words of greeting, or an occasional encouraging smile, or even a friendly grasp of the hand, from his earthly sovereign, but would never be so presump-

* 'Mysticism,' by Rev. A. B. Sharpe, pp. 93, 97.

tuous as to expect to be invited into his private apartments, or to sit down at his table, and would certainly not dream of being caressed and familiarly loved, so we are naturally inclined to think that God in Heaven will be exalted far too infinitely above us to treat with us individually and familiarly and with real tenderness and affection.

But the astounding fact is the very reverse of our imaginings. So far from standing aloof from us, He will unite Himself in the most inconceivably intimate manner to each soul, and be 'all-in-all' even to the least of the Blessed.

When we recall what God does for us, day by day, even in this land of exile, such extraordinary intimacy should evoke no surprise. If, in Holy Communion, God gives Himself to each individual soul, wholly and entirely, Body, Blood, Soul, and Divinity, just as though no other creature existed, and this while we are yet sinners, and *in via*, how much more readily and in how much more admirable a manner will He not give Himself to us when we are purified from sin and *in patria?* Listen to the following description, by the late Bishop Hedley, concerning the close personal union between the soul and its God in Holy Communion:

'In this Sacrament, worthily received, the holy and powerful personality of Jesus comes into contact with the being of a man, into a nearness that did not exist before. It is a contact of power or of "virtue" in the scholastic phrase; faculty affects faculty; intellect affects intellect; will touches will; holiness seeks room for itself; humility and obedience flow in like a tide; love and piety penetrate like the morning light. Christ is in us like a diffused aroma, influencing, bracing, intensifying, sanctifying all the springs of spiritual life, and even natural life. It is difficult to put any limit to this all-embracing union of Jesus with the soul and heart, except that of a man's own receptive action. If a man responds, Jesus stints not His communication.'*

Marvellous indeed is such intimacy; but immeasurably more marvellous still must be the intimacy between the glorified soul and its Divine Spouse in the heavenly courts,

* 'A Spiritual Retreat,' p. 135.

when the Divine Presence, filling and flooding the soul, will no longer be hidden away under the sacramental species, but will be manifest and dazzling in its infinite beauty and splendour.* Nothing is so magnificent as God. If we are attracted by glory, we shall find in Him infinite glory; if we have a taste for

* 'L'amour opère alors, par voie de transformation, une telle ressemblance entre eux, qu'ils sont à la fois l'un et l'autre, et que les deux sont un. Et cela se comprend parce que dans l'union et la transformation d'amour, l'un donne possession de soi à l'autre, chacun s'abandonne, se livre et s'échange pour l'autre; c'est ainsi que chacun vit dans l'autre, et que l'un est en même temps l'autre, cependant que les deux sont un, par transformation d'amour. C'est bien là ce que saint Paul veut faire comprendre quand il dit de lui-même: "*Vivo autem, jam non ego, vivit vero in me Christus*" (Gal. ii. 20). . . . Sa vie est plus divine qu'humaine, ce qui lui permet de dire qu'il ne vit plus, lui, mais le Christ en lui. De sorte que selon cette ressemblance par transformation, nous pouvons dire que sa vie et celle de Jésus-Christ étaient une même vie dans l'union d'amour. C'est bien là ce qui s'accomplira de façon parfaite au ciel, dans la vie divine, pour tous ceux qui auront mérité de se voir en Dieu. Transformés en Dieu, ils vivront la vie de Dieu, et non la leur propre, bien qu'ils vivront aussi de leur vie, puisque la vie de Dieu sera leur vie.'—(St. John of the Cross, in the very last and most up-to-date French translation, by Chanoine H. Hoornaert, 1918, p. 105.)

the beautiful, we shall find nothing so beautiful as He is. Do we seek abundance? He is rich in everything. If we love faithful hearts, who can offer a constancy equal to His? Do we wish to be led by severity or by sweetness? Nothing is so terrible as His power; nothing so reassuring as His pity. Do we need consolation in affliction, or a guide in prosperity? From Him alone we receive all joy in good fortune, all alleviation in grief. Reason, then, demands that we should love Him in whom the most perfect gifts are found.

In this connection we may perhaps quote the following striking passage from Cardinal Newman:

'I believe, and confess, and adore the incomprehensible God, as being infinitely more wonderful, resourceful, and immense than this universe, which I see. I look into the depth of space, in which the stars are scattered about, and I understand that I should be millions upon millions of years creeping along from one end of it to the other, if a bridge were thrown across it. I consider the overwhelming variety, richness, intricacy of God's work; the elements, principles, laws, results which go to make it up. I try to recount the multitudes of kinds of knowledge of sciences, and of arts, of which it can be made the subject. And I know I should be ages upon ages in learning everything that is to be learned about this world, supposing me to have the power of learning it at all. And new sciences would come to light, at present unsuspected, as fast as I had mastered the old, and the conclusions of to-day would be nothing more than starting-points of to-morrow. And I see, moreover, and the *more* I examine it, the *more* I shall understand the marvellous beauty of these works of His hands. And so I might begin again, after this material universe, and find a new world of knowledge, higher and more wonderful, in His intellectual creations, His angels, and other spirits, and men. But all, all that is in these worlds, high and low, are *but an atom* compared with the grandeur, the height and depth and the glory on which His saints are gazing, in their contemplation of God. It is the occupation of eternity, ever new, inexhaustible, ineffably ecstatic, the stay and the blessedness of existence, thus to drink in and be dissolved in God.' *

Bearing in mind man's intense and insatiable thirst for happiness, it is certainly difficult to understand why 'the desire to be dissolved, and to be with Christ,' should not be more conspicuous and more universal among God's faithful followers. When one considers, in the first place, who God is, and, in the second place, His promise to give Himself to each faithful soul, with even greater fullness and completeness than a bridegroom gives himself to his bride: 'I am thy reward, exceeding great' (Gen. xv. 1), surely one might expect the words of David, or at least their equivalent, to be constantly on every Christian's lips: 'As the hart panteth after the fountains of water; so my soul panteth after Thee, O my God' (Ps. xli.).

In short, the question we propose to ourselves is this: Granting that what St. John of the Cross says to be true—viz.: 'If the soul had but one single glimpse of the grandeur and the beauty of God, it would not only desire

* 'Meditations and Devotions.' By Cardinal Newman, pp. 588-590.

to die at once, in order to behold Him, but would endure joyfully *a thousand most bitter deaths, to behold Him, even for a* MOMENT,' etc. (vol. ii., p. 57)—how comes it that scarcely anyone is found to be longing and impatient to die, I will not say a thousand most bitter deaths, but so much as *one* single easy death, in order that he may see God, not for a moment merely, but that he may feast upon the heavenly vision securely for all eternity? This is, surely, an extraordinary anomaly.

The explanation generally given of this inconsistency is wholly unsatisfactory. People will answer somewhat as follows: 'Well, the fact is, you see, the whole thing is so uncertain. Nobody really knows whether he be deserving of love or of hate (Eccles. ix. 1). We can never feel absolutely sure of going to the right place,' and so forth. But, in sober truth, this is no real explanation at all, for experience itself proves, beyond a doubt, that one may be brimming over with joy and exultation at the mere prospect of a happiness the *source of which is by no means absolutely secure.*

Suffer me to illustrate my contention by an example.

I once became acquainted with an attractive and intelligent young German, whom, for the purpose of my illustration, I will call Fritz. I got to know him very well, so, observing him for some time to be low and dejected and out of sorts, I ventured at last to ask him the cause of his melancholy. After a little hesitation he told me, in confidence, that the fact was he was over head and shoulders in love with 'the most beautiful and the most charming and accomplished *mädchen* in all the world,' who dwelt on the banks of the Rhine, and that his one wish in life was to marry her. But, unfortunately, there were difficulties in the way; and her parents absolutely refused to sanction the match, etc. In consequence of this, for many months the young man kept on brooding over his hard fate, so that melancholy claimed him for her own.

Then, all at once, there came a sudden and complete change. I remember it very well. It was on a bright, beautiful sunny day towards the end of May. Though Fritz was not living with me at the time, yet he got into the house somehow, and then, without knocking or craving admittance in his usual way, he flung open my sitting-room door and rushed in without any ceremony, clapping his hands and dancing up and down in an uncontrollable ecstasy, crying out: 'Thank God! It is all right; everything arranged. My happy cup is overflowing.'

'No,' I said (taking care to keep quite calm), 'no, you mean that your cup of happiness is brimming over.'

But he was in no mood to bear correcting. Again he repeated: 'My happy cup is full—over full—running over. I—am at last accepted! She will be mine! for ever mine! all mine! mine alone!'

In short, the wedding had been at last happily arranged, and he was to marry this paragon of perfection.

The following morning I accompanied my young and enthusiastic friend to the station and saw him off by the train. I must confess that I have never in all my life come across anyone so radiantly happy, or anyone whose happiness so shone and glowed on every feature. His boyish face seemed to be quite lit up and was wreathed with happy smiles, while his eyes sparkled with pleasure and excitement, and his very voice seemed to have grown tender and more amorous. As he sat in a corner of the railway carriage waiting for the train to start, I said to him: 'Now, my dear Fritz, do not be too sure. You know that "There's many a slip between the cup and the lip." '

He looked anxious and said: 'What *do* you mean?' I replied: 'The *mädchen* may die before you can reach her. Or your train may get smashed up between here and the coast. Or the boat carrying you over the sea may founder, with all on board. In fact, *you are not absolutely sure* of ever seeing your *fiancée* again.'

'True,' he responded; 'I am not, of course, *absolutely* sure, but I am quite sure enough to make my heart bound with joy. The chances are quite good enough to make me feel that I am now in heaven, and perfectly happy.' Then he threw up his hands and exclaimed: 'I am in heaven; I am already in heaven, *now*. Oh! What will it be when I can actually clasp her to my heart!"

Here, then, is a case in which many and

most undoubted risks have to be faced—a case in which a hundred different accidents may happen to interfere with and even entirely to frustrate the realization of his dream; yet, observe, they do not destroy or even seriously diminish his joyous exultation and jubilant happiness. Now, if this be true in this and in thousands of similar cases, in the *natural* order, how comes it that certain unavoidable risks of salvation should prove so destructive of a like exultation in the *supernatural* order? It is hard to assign a reason, and seems somewhat illogical and absurd.

Besides, it should be borne in mind that the dangers that threaten an earthly lover ought to inspire much greater fear and anxiety, since they, indeed, depend upon circumstances over which he has no control. The aspirant after heavenly joys, on the contrary, knows, with the certainty of Divine faith, that nothing can rob *him* of *his* prize but his own infidelity. He is fully conscious that the only person who has so much as the power to wreck all his hopes is HIMSELF!

Hence, in spite of what so many say, I

contend that the bare possibility of losing Heaven and of forfeiting one's claim to the eternal possession of God cannot, of itself, account for the apathy and indifference of which we complain.

Furthermore, hope is a theological virtue. We are bound to hope; and most of us, if we are generously and loyally trying to serve God, have very good reasons to hope, since we feel a moral certainty of being in a state of grace; consequently, it seems to me that we should be literally on fire with the desire of beholding our King, in all His glory. Not only is the prize at which we aim infinitely higher than that which is looked forward to by the most favoured earthly lover, but our chances of winning it are also immeasurably more solidly established and far more securely founded, yet, strange to say, we are not half so beside ourselves with joy.

Most of the Saints seemed to have been filled with a great longing for Heaven. We read of many a one who, on being informed that he was dying, was heard to cry out in the greatest joy and expectancy: 'Laetatus sum in his quae dicta sunt mihi—in domum

Domini ibimus.' Others, we are assured, like St. Martin, have actually expressed themselves willing to prolong their earthly course, if God saw it to be expedient, as though such an act of self-sacrifice were *an act of the most consummate heroism.** In the case of St. Ignatius, the martyr, so little did the prospect of his cruel death check his longing to be with his Divine Master that he was ready to suffer anything to secure such a delight, and cried out, in the fervour of his heart: 'Omnia tormenta diaboli in me veniant, dummodo Christo fruar!' 'Oh!' exclaims St. Teresa, 'if we were utterly detached, how the pain caused by living always away from God would temper the fear of death with the desire of enjoying the true life. Sometimes I consider that if a person like myself [St. Teresa, being a great Saint, thought herself, of course, the worst of sinners] frequently feels her banishment so acutely, what must have been the feelings of the Saints! What must St. Paul and the Mag-

* 'Martinus ita Deum orabat: Domine, si adhuc populo tuo sum necessarius, non recuso laborem' (Brev., die 11 Novembris).

dalene, and others like them, have suffered, in whom the fire of the love of God had grown so strong! Their life must have been a continual martyrdom.'*

'Who truly and ardently loves another,' observes the learned Cardinal Bellarmin,† 'cannot endure with patience the absence of the beloved; but, whether he eats or drinks or whatsoever else he does, he is always thinking of, and sighing for, and desiring the company of the loved one. Even while he sleeps, his thoughts are about her, and he sees and converses with her in his dreams. And, if such be the case [continues the great Cardinal] with those whose hearts are on fire with the love of one who is mortal and

* 'Life,' p. 161.

† As my translation is a very 'free' one, perhaps I had better give the Cardinal's actual words: 'Qui vere et ex corde diligit, non potest patienter tolerare absentiam dilecti; sed sive comedat, sive bibat, sive quid aliud agat, semper dilectum cogitat, et cogitando suspirat, et plorat. Et si forte dormiat, illum quoque somniando videt, et cum eo confabulatur. Et si haec accidunt iis, qui amore capti sunt rerum mortalium et foedarum; quid illi facient, qui amore capti sunt pulchritudinis infinitae et sempiternae' (*De Gemitu Columbae*, l. ii., chap. x., p. 182).

imperfect and unworthy, who shall describe the passionate longing and the insatiable thirst of those whose hearts have become enamoured with a Beauty that is infinite and uncreated and eternal !'

The fact of the matter is, we do not love God half enough, nor do we sufficiently occupy our minds with the thought of the wholly inconceivably magnificent rewards which He has prepared for those who love Him. If only we kept this startling truth more frequently in mind, not only should we appreciate our privilege far more intensely, but we would experience a profound happiness, such as the world cannot give, even amid all the trials and vicissitudes of life, and would be constantly buoyed up by the brightest anticipations of so glorious a future. Even death itself would lose its terrors, and the present world its attractions, and, like another St. Ignatius de Loyola, we would exclaim, with perfect sincerity: 'Quam sordet tellus dum coelum intueor.'

# CONTENTS

# LIFE EVERLASTING

## CHAPTER I

## OUR HOME ABOVE

### I

This world is all a fleeting show
  For man's illusion given ;
The smiles of joy, the tears of woe,
Deceitful shine, deceitful flow—
  There's nothing true but Heaven.

T. MOORE.

EVERY Catholic who is leading an ordinarily good life fully expects, and with good reason, to be saved. He knows, with the certainty of Divine faith, that he must necessarily, and under every conceivable circumstance, spend the whole of eternity either amid the unutterable delights of Heaven or else amid the raging fires of Hell. And, as he most certainly does not intend nor expect to be sent to Hell, we may readily infer that he expects and, in a measure, counts upon being received into Heaven.

As he resolutely refrains from mortal sin and steadfastly struggles to avoid even deliberate venial offences, he is reasonably cheered and buoyed up by a well-grounded confidence that he will, one day (not through his own merits indeed, but through the infinite mercy of God), actually enter into the heavenly courts, to enjoy an endless existence of the most perfect and unclouded happiness. This will lead him often to make such reflections as the following: 'Beyond this world of matter, beyond this universe of suns and moons and gleaming stars, of rushing comets and flashing meteors, there lies another world, another universe, immeasurably vaster, incalculably more wonderful and admirable, as well as infinitely more magnificent and beautiful, towards which I am hastening without pause or cessation. Within a few years, without the shadow of a doubt, but possibly in a few weeks or days or hours, I shall find myself there living an immortal life amid totally different surroundings, with totally different friends and companions, and with quite other interests and occupations. This is not a mere hope, nor is it pure fancy or idle imagination, but a most solidly established fact, and as undeniable as my existence at this very hour. Just as I have seen others depart and quit home and fatherland and friends for that "undiscovered country from whose bourn no traveller returns," so, in an indescribably brief time, I too shall bid an eternal farewell to this world, in order to take up my permanent abode in the other.'

Though it is true that all thoughtful men will sometimes entertain such solemn thoughts, and will freely express such convictions, yet, strange to say, but very few seem sufficiently interested to make any serious inquiries as to the nature and character of that marvellous region, 'not made with hands,' towards which they are ever hastening, whether they advert to the fact or not, at such lightning-like speed.

When a man is about to leave his own country, for the first time, to settle in some distant and more favoured land, we find that he is naturally anxious to learn all he can about his new home. If, for example, he be appointed Governor of one of our flourishing colonies, such as Victoria, or New South Wales, or Tasmania, he at once seeks to acquaint himself with its extent, its configuration, its climate and population. He makes a genuine effort and is ready to take some trouble to find out the character of the people, their language, and their manners and customs. In short, he manifests a strong desire to learn all that he can of the country or the colony in which he is destined to spend the next few years of his earthly life.

Now, this is most natural and most reasonable. In fact, it is so completely in accordance with prudence and good sense that it is very hard to understand why the great majority of men seem so little interested and so little anxious to know more about the great invisible world—so very near at hand—in which they are fated to live, not for a few years only, but for ever and for ever.

That wondrous and invisible world is even now awaiting them. Its existence is past dispute. It is far more real, more permanent and lasting, and more firmly established than the solid earth, upon which we now stand. For this rude material earth will one day dissolve and pass away, but Heaven shall never pass away.

> The cloud-capped towers, the gorgeous palaces,
> The solemn temples, the great globe itself,
> Yes ! all which it inherits, shall dissolve;
> And, like an insubstantial pageant faded,
> Leave not a rack behind.
>
> SHAKESPEARE.

And, what is more, it is equally certain that, after a few more seasons have come and gone, God will send His angel of death to conduct us to His unspeakably happy Home above.

> The world recedes; it disappears !
> Heav'n opens on my eyes ! My ears
> With sounds seraphic ring;
> Lend, lend your wings ! I mount, I fly !
> O grave, where is thy victory ?
> O death, where is thy sting ?
>
> POPE.

Of course, it may be objected that it is useless to spend time in contemplating the future abode of the elect, because we can know so little about it. We reply, It is true, certainly, that we cannot offer an *adequate* account, because no human mind can conceive and no earthly language can convey any accurate idea of the exquisite delights which God has prepared for those who love Him and serve Him loyally: if indeed these delights were *such as we might describe in human language, they would not be worth seeking.** On the authority of God Himself, we know that 'eye hath not seen, nor ear heard, neither hath it entered into the heart of man, what things God hath prepared for them that love Him' (1 Cor. ii. 9).

But this does not mean that we can learn nothing. Indeed, both reason and revelation, if properly questioned, will tell us a vast deal more than some persons think, and most certainly far more than is needed to awaken strong desires within the soul, and to set the whole heart on fire with a holy longing 'to be dissolved, and to be with Christ,' if they will but give the matter their serious consideration. Then, let us to the task.

* The so-called 'Spirit-Messages to Mr. Vale Owen,' which occupied many columns in the *Weekly Dispatch*, may be pointed to as affording a good specimen of the nonsensical piffle which results when any attempt is made to give a detailed and minute description of life in another world. Such illusive drivel and profane trifling only disgusts and sickens one. (See *Weekly Dispatch*, November, 1920.)

We may begin by considering that the infallible voice of the Church informs us that our bodies, as well as our souls, are destined to rejoice for ever with God, although both must undergo prodigious changes, in order that they may, in every way, correspond with their new environment. In considering these we will begin by calling attention to the changes to be wrought in the more insignificant portion of our being—viz., our bodies—and then pass on to learn what we can of the changes to be effected in our nobler part—viz., in our spiritual and intellectual souls. 'In a moment, in the twinkling of an eye, at the last trumpet, the dead shall rise again incorruptible, and *we shall be changed*' (1 Cor. xv. 52). Such is the teaching of revelation.

Though the body will be the selfsame body which our soul now informs on earth, and by means of which it is now able to exercise its powers of seeing, hearing, and the rest, yet it will be strengthened, beautified, and richly endowed with supernatural gifts and powers, in a degree wholly beyond the power of the highest imagination to picture.

In order to form some dim estimate of its ravishing beauty, let us set before the eyes of our imagination the most exquisitely beautiful human form that has ever aroused the admiration of the world. It is indeed a work of God, but it would be easy for Him to create a second of the same species, but twice as beautiful, and a third, twice as beautiful as the second, and so on and on, and yet never exhaust His power of rendering it more beautiful still. Now, while we admit God to possess such infinite powers, our next concern will be to form some idea as to the extent to which He will exercise these powers in fashioning our risen bodies. In order to arrive at a satisfactory answer, we shall find it useful to ask ourselves three fundamental questions:

1. *How* is the risen body formed ?
2. For *what purpose* is it formed ?
3. What *position* and *place* is it destined to occupy, when it is formed ?

In dealing with the first question, we may begin by considering that the bodies we now have are no doubt, in a certain sense, the work of God, and exceedingly 'wonderfully and fearfully made' (Psalms), but they are in no sense the *direct and immediate* work of God. A human body now is formed very gradually and slowly, by the operation of certain laws which the Creator has established. And *because* it is produced by finite and very imperfect instruments, the result also is always more or less defective and imperfect. A thousand different causes may influence the life of an infant during the time of gestation, and interfere with the absolute and complete perfection of the material form which at last emerges into light. And, even after birth, there are innumerable circumstances which may militate against its full and due development, so that an absolutely perfect and an absolutely beautiful body 'without spot or wrinkle' (Eph. v. 27) is rarely, if ever (*and probably never*) produced. Now, none of these objections can be urged in the case of the risen body. There is nothing, and *there can be nothing*, to hinder or to interfere in any way whatsoever with its perfection. The risen body is not a product of nature at all, nor the result of the operation of any physical laws. It is not produced by the slow and tedious process of conception and gestation, but is the direct and immediate effect of the Divine will. It is God Who calls it into being. It is God Who raises it up. He, Who is infinitely perfect, produces it instantly, and by His direct *fiat*. Consequently, being His own and personal work, it will bear the impress of His Divine hands, and reflect the beauty of His own infinite perfection, to an extent impossible for us now to realize. Its loveliness will startle and delight us, for it will come before us as *a perfect work of a perfect Artist*, without flaw or blemish, spot or wrinkle.

Even in this world we are able to appreciate the difference between the work of a consummate artist and the clumsy attempts of a mere pupil. Whether it be in the construction of a work of art, or of some mechanical contrivance, we can always detect the work of a master-hand. A watch, made by the master, is valued above that which is produced by a common apprentice. A painting by a Raphael or a Titian stands on a higher level, and will fetch a bigger price, than that which is produced by even the best of their pupils. If, then, such appreciable differences exist even among the works of different men, all of whom stand much on the same level, such differences will be infinitely greater still when the master-hand is no other than the Hand of God, and when the Artist is the Infinite, the Uncreated and the Omnipotent.

Hence, the risen body, *because the direct work of God,** will possess a perfection, a charm, a fascination, as well as a beauty and a splendour, utterly inconceivable to us now, and wholly beyond the highest flight of the most soaring imagination to reach. This brings us to the *second question*—viz., For what purpose is it formed ?

That there must be a limitless difference between the risen body and the corruptible body must be inferred also from a consideration of the extent of the difference in the

* 'Anima sicut immediate a Deo creata est, ita immediate a Deo corpori iterato unietur sine aliqua operatione angelorum. Similiter etiam gloriam corporis Ipse faciet absque ministerio angelorum sicut et animam immediate glorificat' (St. Thomas, iii., Q. lxxvi., Art. 3).

God is God. Hence, it is evident that it must be formed on wholly different principles to our present bodies, which are intended to suffer for a few fleeting years and then to fall into decay.

Now, no sane man will bestow as much thought and care upon an object which is to last but a day or an hour as he will bestow upon an object which is to last him all his *purpose* for which each is made. The poor, weak body, which we now have, 'cometh forth like a flower, and is destroyed, and fleeth as a shadow, and never continueth in the same state' (Job xiv. 2). It is even declared to be 'a load upon the soul which presseth down the mind, that museth upon many things' (Wis. ix. 15). Indeed, it is so formed that it is liable to suffer and endure endless miseries, trials, and afflictions. As a punishment for sin, it is made subject to extremes of heat and cold, as well as to hunger, thirst, want, and nakedness.



together to form a temporary hut, or he may construct a decent shelter from the boughs of trees, but it would never occur to him to design and construct an elaborate mansion or a lordly castle, with moat and portcullis and massive outer walls, and all the rest, merely to serve so transitory a purpose. He would be content with a folding tent, if he were making no stay. If, on the contrary, he were planning a residence in which to pass the rest of his days, he would spare no pains to make it as elegant, as strong, and as magnificent and spacious as he could. On somewhat similar grounds, the body, in which the glorified soul is to dwell *for ever*, will be fashioned in a very different manner to the body which begins to corrupt as soon as it is born, and which, even with the greatest care, can seldom be preserved for so much even as a hundred years. In short, as eternity differs from time, so will the imperishable body, *made for Eternity*, differ from the corruptible body, *made merely for Time*.

Hence, once these premises are granted, we can see by the light of reason itself that the risen body must be constructed on wholly different lines to our present bodies.

Further, the earthly body is so built up that its parts may hold together only for a few years at most. It is so put together that Time's effacing fingers soon put an end to its brief career. It is constructed, *designedly*, to last but for a short period. On the other hand, the risen body receives from the Hand of God an existence which is destined to be eternal. It is so made that it may flourish for ever and ever, so long as God is God. Hence, it is evident that it must be formed on wholly different principles to our present bodies, which are intended to suffer for a few fleeting years and then to fall into decay.

Now, no sane man will bestow as much thought and care upon an object which is to last but a day or an hour as he will bestow upon an object which is to last him all his life. A benighted traveller, who finds himself compelled to spend a night or two on his way to his destination, may put a few planks together to form a temporary hut, or he may construct a decent shelter from the boughs of trees, but it would never occur to him to design and construct an elaborate mansion or a lordly castle, with moat and portcullis and massive outer walls, and all the rest, merely to serve so transitory a purpose. He would be content with a folding tent, if he were making no stay. If, on the contrary, he were planning a residence in which to pass the rest of his days, he would spare no pains to make it as elegant, as strong, and as magnificent and spacious as he could. On somewhat similar grounds, the body, in which the glorified soul is to dwell *for ever*, will be fashioned in a very different manner to the body which begins to corrupt as soon as it is born, and which, even with the greatest care, can seldom be preserved for so much even as a hundred years. In short, as eternity differs from time, so will the imperishable body, *made for Eternity*, differ from the corruptible body, *made merely for Time*.

This brings us to the third question which we have to ask ourselves: What position and place is the glorified body to occupy when once it is formed? The earthly body lives on gross material food, and dwells amid the rude and uncouth elements of this rough world. It shares, with millions of others, an earthly existence, in which clothing and shelter and long hours of unconscious sleep are absolutely necessary. All its surroundings are common, and often sordid and unhealthy, and its occupations frequently dreary, dangerous, and degrading. In a word, it passes its years, and labours and toils in an environment which demands from the body nothing better nor more comely or more elegant than what we know it actually possesses.

But Heaven! Oh! Heaven, with all its undreamed-of splendour, and unrivalled glory, and unparalleled magnificence, neither would nor could admit within its celestial walls anything so unlovely, gross, and sordid as a body such as we have to be satisfied with on earth. From the very condition of things, the risen body *must* be, in all respects, fully worthy of the heavenly city in which it is destined to dwell. It *must be fitted and arrayed and rendered in every sense worthy to rank with the glorious spirits above,* and be made as fair and as resplendent, in its own nature, as they are in theirs. In short, the risen body must be such that the soul, which informs it, may know and feel that it is in complete harmony and conformity with its splendid surroundings. Nay, more, it must be rendered so superlatively beautiful, spotless, and attractive, as to be able even to add something to the general glory and adornment of its new home. It must scintillate and sparkle like a new star, in the firmament of Heaven, and its very presence must be so lovely and so joy-giving as to rejoice and gladden every beholder. In other words, it must be so clothed and adorned by God as to be, in every sense, a *worthy citizen of the supernal City of God, whose splendour outrivals all thought and all possible conception.*

So soon as we begin to form a just idea of the unparalleled glory of Heaven, it is quite enough for us to realize that the body is created to occupy a place there, to enable us to draw the conclusion that the said body must be a totally different thing, at least in all its attributes, senses, faculties, and powers, from the body with which we are now acquainted.

A renowned general, returning from the wars, would never think of attending a royal levee clad in a shooting jacket, gaiters, and a pair of muddy boots; no young lady would dare to present herself at Court in a costume which she puts on when she goes for a ramble over the rocks. In fact, even in this world, we realize that some regard must be had to circumstances and surroundings. And if this be according to reason, custom, and common sense, it surely forms a very strong argument in proof of our contention that there must be a gigantic difference between the earthly body (sometimes spoken of as 'the garment of the soul'), which we wear now, and the royal robes, which we shall wear before the Great White Throne in Heaven.

To aid us in our attempts to take in the situation, let us consider one of Heaven's glorious citizens—namely, the great Archangel Gabriel—as he is depicted in the inspired Book of Daniel. We cannot, of course, see a spirit with our corporal eyes, so the

2

apparition which Daniel beheld must have been far less soul-stirring than the reality would have been, could it have been perceived. But even this wraith or 'shade' of the Archangel which the Prophet did gaze upon so terrified and unnerved him that he sank down to the ground, buried his face in the dust, and could not utter a word. Yea, the very joints of his bones were loosened, as he himself tells us. To accommodate himself to the requirements of the situation, this splendid creature of God took the form of a man. He is described as 'a man clothed in linen, and whose loins were girded with the finest gold. His body was like the chrysolite, and his face as the appearance of lightning, and his eyes as burning lamps, and his arms, and all downward, even to the feet, like in appearance to glittering brass. And his voice was like the voice of a multitude' (Dan. x. 5, 6). The Prophet then goes on to describe the effect which this heavenly appearance had upon him: 'And there remained no strength in me, and the appearance of my countenance was changed in me, and I fainted away, and retained no strength.' At the sound of his voice, 'I lay in a consternation upon my face, and close to the ground.' And at the sight of him, 'my joints were loosened, and no strength remained in me' (Dan. x. 8, 9, 16).

Though the mere 'shade' of a single Archangel could throw even an intrepid and saintly prophet* into the depth of abject fear, so that he could not even converse with his celestial visitor, or feel at ease in his presence, yet we know that the very least and last of 'the just made perfect' in Heaven will not only live in the naked presence of the Archangel Gabriel, but of countless other spirits, quite as great as he. In fact, if ever we are so fortunate as to enter into that glorious abode, we shall not only stand undismayed in the presence of the Archangel Gabriel, but we shall mix with and be the constant and familiar companions and fellow-citizens of innumerable other Angels and Archangels, quite as great and majestic and

* So intrepid, that he was ready to face the lions in their den, rather than offend God; and so saintly, that his feast is commemorated in the Roman Martyrology on July 21.

as superbly beautiful as he is. So that, both in body and mind, we must be so constituted as not only to endure the sight without being, Daniel-like, paralyzed with fear and terrified out of our senses, but so as to glory and rejoice in it, while remaining completely at our ease. How greatly, then, must the risen differ from the corruptible body !

Far more ! It is essential that we should be so formed as to remain confident and happy, and on the most intimate and affectionate terms, not only with Archangels, but with each and all of the countless myriads of other Blessed Spirits, who are much more exalted than even the Archangels themselves. Let us, who are, after all, 'heirs to the kingdom of Heaven,' remember that the inspired Scriptures speak of no less than nine different choirs of Blessed Spirits, and that of these the Angels and the Archangels are the very least and lowest. We *begin* with (1) Angels, and (2) Archangels, but then we soar above them, in an ever-ascending scale, first of all to the Principalities, then to the Powers, then to the Virtues, and so on to the Dominations, to the Thrones, and the Cherubim, and finally (nearest of all to God) to the Seraphim themselves!

Surely, with the picture of Daniel before us, prostrate and terrified in presence of a single Angel, we shall realize that our mortal frame will need a good deal of alteration, and a good deal of strengthening and perfecting, before we can be admitted to, and before we can feel at all at home in, the heavenly courts.

This necessity will become all the more evident to us if we consider, further, that each Choir or Order of Angels contains so vast a number* that no man can reckon them, and that, in the opinion of our greatest theologians, like St. Thomas,† each and every member of each of the nine Choirs is a distinct species of itself.

I suppose there is scarcely anything that so fires the imagination, or that so betokens

* 'D. Thom. dicit numerum angelorum incomparabiliter superare numerum substantiarum materialium, idque confirmat auctoritate S. Dionysii.'

† 'Impossibile est esse duos angelos unius speciei. . . . Perfectio naturae angelicae requirit multiplicationem specierum, non autem multiplicationem individuorum una specie.'—St. Thomas Aquinas.

and attests the limitless resources of divine wisdom and power, as this most fascinating view of the great St. Thomas. It is positively bewildering to think of each individual Angel as a distinct species in himself. For it means that we shall, as it were, discover a *totally new* world of beauty, and splendour, and glory wherever our eyes rest; and that as we pass from the contemplation of one Angel to another we shall be more and more filled with wonder and admiration, and more and more ravished by the continuous fresh proofs of God's unlimited fecundity and skill, in creating such an exhaustless variety of distinct specimens of loveliness, without ever exhausting or repeating Himself. To Him be all honour and glory for ever !

Further, it must be borne in mind that the City of God above is totally different from an earthly city also in this, that every one of its countless citizens will know each other, and enjoy each other's society. In this world one's powers as well as one's opportunities are so exceedingly limited that the vast multitudes filling a great city remain wholly unknown to us. Though we may have been residing within its walls all our life, and though millions may be dwelling all around us, yet our really intimate friends and acquaintances and our personal relations form but a negligible quantity, and the merest fraction of the whole. Of the overwhelming majority, who may be seen sauntering through their gardens, riding in the public parks, or driving through the streets, we know practically nothing whatsoever, and perhaps care less. But in Heaven we shall know, love, and feel the keenest interest in every single one of its inhabitants. There will be no strangers and no foreigners there, for the immense myriad, which no man can number, will form but one great and united family, bound close together by a thousand ties, mutually honoured, esteemed, and appreciated, and loved beyond measure.

And even though great differences will undoubtedly exist, for we are told that 'the Blessed shall differ from one another, as stars differ from stars in glory,' yet these differences will not create any divisions nor exclusive circles nor special parties or classes, as they do in this world, but the highest and the lowest—as children of the same Father—will understand one another, and be more closely united, and even feel a greater joy in each other's presence, than any two lovers ever yet did in this sad world. And how much that means, who shall declare?

Though these are solemn facts, yet the difficulty is fully to realize that we are treating of stern realities, and not of dreams and phantoms: yes, the difficulty is thoroughly to convince ourselves that such ordinary creatures as ourselves are shortly to be translated into such an absolutely different state of existence, and that all this beauty and splendour is indeed for us. At first blush it seems all far too good to be true or even possible. The idea intoxicates, overwhelms, and stuns us. Yet, the more calmly and the more carefully we weigh the arguments and the proofs, the more steadfastly and irresistibly is their glorious truth borne in upon us. To every one of us is the divine invitation extended. So that there is not one but may hear, in a short time, if only he be faithful, the entrancing words, foretold by St. Matthew, 'Come, ye blessed of My

Father, possess ye the Kingdom *prepared for you,* from the foundation of the world' (Matt. xxv. 34). 'He that shall overcome shall possess these things, and I will be his God; and he shall be My son' (Apoc. xxi. 7).

We may well conclude the present chapter with these divine and consoling promises ringing in our soul.

## CHAPTER II

## EARTH AND HEAVEN CONTRASTED

Some day in Spring,
  When earth is fair and glad,
And sweet birds sing
  And fewest hearts are sad—
Shall I die then ?
Ah me ! no matter when;
  I know it will be sweet
To leave the homes of men,
  And rest beneath the sod,
To kneel and kiss Thy feet
  In Thy home, O my God !

FATHER RYAN.

THE resurrection of the body is quite one of the most thrilling and startling doctrines that have been revealed to us. Nor is it one we are at all likely to forget. Each one of us makes an explicit act of faith in that wonderful dogma every time we recite the Creed. Furthermore, it is a truth which is not only most clearly and most emphatically proclaimed by Christ Himself, and by St. Paul and St. John, and by the Universal Church, but it is likewise a truth of which we are perpetually being put in mind, by even the most ordinary and constant movements and changes ever going on in the physical world around us; changes which we must surely suppose to have been intentionally designed and arranged by the thoughtful providence of Him who is just as surely the Author of Nature as He is the Author of grace and of glory.

What is more regular than the perpetual alternation of night and day? Yet, to any reflecting mind, what a beautiful image this sets before us of our death and resurrection! Every twenty-four hours the bright and gladsome day, so full of life and movement, in forest, field, and fallow, comes to an end—perishes—dies—and as it were sinks into the darkness of the grave. As the soul leaves the body at death, so the sun, the veritable soul of Nature, and its very source of vigour and activity, leaves the world, and sinks down in the West, while over the entire visible world is thrown the deep black funeral pall of night. And *then*, the stillness and the darkness and almost the silence of death seems to brood over all.

Yet, in a few hours, there comes a glorious resurrection. The whole heavens awaken. Once more they are aglow with brightness and beauty. All Nature revives. The world is astir, once again, with its millions of active, industrious, energetic workers. Blinds are drawn; shutters are removed; shops are opened, and streets and squares fill with multitudes of busy and interested inhabitants, whose echoing footsteps, breaking on the ear, tell us that the impetuous stream of life now flows again, and that the heart of the great city has once more begun to beat—in short, admonishing us, as it were, that the world has again *risen from the dead.* The blazing sun steeps the earth in a sea of golden splendour; it gleams and shimmers on the running waters of river and stream; it sparkles on the playing fountains in a thousand prismatic colours; it adorns every wandering cloud with all the variegated hues of the rainbow; it stains vast air-spaces with the daintiest and most ethereal blue, and warms and stirs the blood in man and beast, till it dances along every artery and vein, and brings vigour and health into every limb. Not only does it chase away the darkness, but it seems to infuse feeling and strength and power into all upon which it shines. In short, it simply transforms the dull earth, and sets it before our astonished eyes as a superb panorama, so instinct with new life as almost to persuade us that some magic change—some mysterious resurrection—had actually taken place.

Or consider the Seasons, from the same point of view. What better image of death shall we find anywhere than in Winter? The gorgeous Summer, with all its wealth of leaf and blossom, fruit and flower, its umbrageous forests and dancing streams, its carolling birds, its lowing herds, and humming insects, suggests the joys and delights of delectable life and health. But, alas! it endures but for a season. Then Winter comes, like an approaching death. And now, behold the change! The leaves are fallen. The streams are frozen. Nothing but arid, naked stems and bare and rigid branches are to be seen where but lately glowed a thousand differently coloured flowers and fruits. The entire earth seems dead and cold and hard, and as rigid, stiff, and inanimate as a corpse, from which all life has departed.

Yet, even here there is a speedy resurrection awaited. For no sooner does the Spring appear than there is a call—a call, like an angel's trumpet, that all Nature seems to heed and to obey: 'Arise, ye dead; awake from sleep! Live once again!' And behold! the entire scene undergoes a most miraculous change. The face of Nature, so cold, so irresponsive and expressionless, becomes again instinct with life, and hills and valleys smile in comeliness and beauty. The earth, that lay dismal and inert, like a ghastly corpse, has come forth from its shroud of snow, has shaken off its winding-sheets of glittering frost, and has risen beautiful and enchanting, as a bride adorned for her bridegroom.

We have a still more striking image of death and resurrection in the seed that falls to the ground, and dies truly, but only to rise up again, in the far more beautiful form of flower or fruit. As we consign the bodies of our beloved relations and friends to the earth, and there allow them to fall to pieces, so do we also lay the seed in the ground, to disintegrate and corrupt; but just as the seed corrupts, only to give birth to a higher form of life—that is to say, to a life of exquisite beauty and loveliness—so we are reminded that the bodies of our dead die, only to revive again, and to return to an immeasurably higher form of life. Every blushing rose, every sweet-scented lily, in fact, every single specimen of fragrant and lovely flower that meets our gaze, in field or forest, is in very truth a risen body. It is the 'glorified body,' the risen body of some dead and buried seed. 'Senseless man, that which thou sowest is not quickened except it die first. And that which thou sowest, thou sowest *not the body that shall be*, but bare grain, as of wheat. *But God giveth it a body as He will:* and to every seed its proper body'; 'One is the glory of the sun, another the glory of the moon, and another the glory of the stars' (1 Cor. xv. 36-38, 41).

Thus, in one way or another, all Nature reminds us of the wonderful doctrine of the resurrection. All fills and cheers our minds with joyous anticipations of a glorious life to come. Nor are these reminders confined to the insensible and vegetable world. The animal kingdom affords even yet more beautiful images. Consider, for instance, the transformation of the somewhat repulsive and ugly caterpillar into the beautiful downy moth, or into the gorgeously painted butterfly. The poor little crawling, creeping grub may be seen ravenously devouring the common leaves of its favourite shrub, until its brief course of caterpillar life is run. It then spins its own cocoon, and assumes the form of a chrysalis. The chrysalis, which in appearance closely resembles a tiny Egyptian mummy, and is quite as helpless, and as motionless, puts us strongly in mind of a dead body. Yet, all the while, though without any external sign, the wonders of a splendid resurrection are preparing, and before many weeks are passed, the tomb-like chrysalis opens, and, not the crawling ugly caterpillar, but a gorgeously painted butterfly emerges, with outspread wings, all aglow with a hundred vivid tints, sparkling and shimmering like priceless gems in the limpid sunlight. Not only is its body and its dull drab dress entirely transformed, but its life also and occupation are changed. No longer confined to the ground, it springs aloft into the scented air, and wings its independent way wherever fancy leads. *Before,* it was restricted in its movements, and could advance but slowly and with feeble footsteps; but *now* the spacious earth is its home, and it may wander, at will, over hill and valley and through forest or glen. Some such thoughts as these must have been in the mind of Dante when he penned the following beautiful lines:

> O superbi Cristiani miseri, lassi,
> Che, della vista della mente infermi
> Fidanza avete ne' ritrosi passi;
> Non vi accorgete che *noi siam vermi*
> *Nati a formar l'angelica farfalla*
> Che vola alla giustizia senza schermi?
>
> DANTE: *Del Purg.*, Cant. X.

The dragon-fly affords us another striking image of the resurrection of the body. Indeed, it seems almost in this case as if God wished to set before us a living picture that should naturally and readily suggest and recall to our minds the marvels of our own future resurrection from the dead, and the life that is to succeed to it, so far wider and so far more extended than our present.

As is well known, the dragon-fly begins its strange career as a tiny egg, laid on the water. From this emerges a sluggish larva, which finds a dismal and confined abode in the waters of pond or lake. After what we may describe as its earthly life, which lasts about a year, it retires into what naturalists term its 'nymph-case,' so suggestive of the tomb. After which it rises (as it were from the grave) and begins a glorious life of freedom and pleasure, with the whole expanse of sunlit country for its inheritance. Tennyson makes a beautiful reference to this in his 'Two Voices':

> To-day I saw the dragon-fly
> Come from the wells, where he did lie.
> An inner impulse rent the veil
> Of his old husk; from head to tail
> Came out clear plates of sapphire mail.
> He dried his wings; like gauze they grew;
> Thro' crofts and pastures wet with dew,
> A living flash of light he flew.

The dragon-fly's dreary life, at first confined within a dark and muddy swamp, followed by so glorious a resurrection, with the whole of the scent-laden heavens and the flower-strewn earth to roam at large in, seems a fitting emblem of the yet more glorious transformation awaiting our own earthly bodies, now grovelling on the earth. If these little aquatic grubs, living in the dismal and muddy swamp, were to be endowed with intellect, and if their future winged state of life could be made known to them by some divine revelation, how greatly would they look forward to its realization, and how happy would they be in their anticipations of so wonderful and of so delightful a future in store for them! Yet, we Christians, though gifted with intelligence, and though assured on the very highest authority of a future infinitely more glorious still, and infinitely more enduring, think but seldom and with very moderate enthusiasm of that wholly supernatural and celestial state.

We watch at the bedside of some dear friend; we witness the gradual ebbing of the tide of earthly life. At last, we see him depart from amongst us. We lay his body, with all reverence and affection, in the grave, and then, with many a heartfelt prayer for the repose of his soul, we withdraw. But we do not sufficiently support and encourage ourselves by recalling the thought of the unutterable glory that awaits him. 'In a moment,' says St. Paul, 'in the twinkling of an eye, at the last trumpet, he shall rise again, and he shall be changed' (1 Cor. xv. 51, 52).

He shall not only rise, but he shall rise perfect, incorruptible, immortal, beautiful beyond compare, and endowed with every possible grace and splendour; a perfect work of art! A *chef-d'œuvre* of God's infinite power and love. No longer will he need food or drink or clothing or protection, or rest and sleep. He stands independent, with all his earthly needs entirely removed. 'Neither can he die any more; for he is equal to the angels, and is a child of God, being a child of the resurrection' (Luke xx. 36). 'Joy everlasting shall be upon his head; he shall obtain joy and gladness, and sorrow and mourning shall flee away' (Isa. li. 11).

Even our temporary abode, the earth, is full of beauty, yet it cannot, for one moment, be compared with what is to come. The saints have loved to contemplate the innocent joys and the social pleasures of this world, in order that, by way of contrast, they might form some notion of the infinitely higher joys and delights of the next.

St. Augustine reasons thus: 'If God bestows such innumerable and such various gifts, *here on earth*, to His friends and enemies alike, how much greater and more innumerable, sweet, and delicious must be the gifts He will bestow upon His friends in *Heaven!* If there are so many enjoyments in the *days of tears*, how many will there be in the *days of the nuptials?* If, in the *prison*, so many pleasures are to be found, how many will there be in the *land of perfect freedom?*'*

'If,' exclaims St. Bernard, 'the land of our exile and the place of our trial be so exquisite, what must be the beauty and the glory of our true Home!' 'Oh!' cries out St. Ignatius, in an ecstasy of wonder and of gratitude, 'how contemptible and how insipid

* 'Si tanta solatia in hac die lacrymarum, quanta conferes in die nuptiarum? Si tanta delectabilia continet carcer, quanta, quaeso continet patria,' etc.—'Soliloquia ad Deum,' cap. xxi.

grow all the pleasures and delights of this world, while we contemplate the ineffable felicity and the ravishing happiness of the next.'

'When this world's goods are reckoned against the gladness above,' writes St. Gregory, 'they are found to be a clog rather than a help. This present life being compared to life eternal, ought rather to be called death than life. For what is the daily failing of our corruption but, as it were, a creeping death? But what tongue is there that can tell, or what understanding that can comprehend, how great is the rejoicing in the city above, where they have part with the choirs of Angels, where they stand with the most blessed spirits before the glory of the Creator, and where they see the Face of God?'*

Even non-Catholics, and indeed men without any faith at all, have realized and been much struck by the lavishness and the generosity with which God has strewn the path of life. Some even go so absurdly far

* From Pope St. Gregory's homily, in the 7th Lesson of the Office for One Martyr.

as to contend that, under favourable circumstances, the present material world can afford us *all the pleasure* and *all the enjoyment* that any reasonable man could wish for. We have an excellent illustration of this in the following lines by the well-known American writer W. R. Greg. Speaking of our present and earthly career, he writes:

'Human life seems like a delicious feast; the most magnificent banquet ever spread by a kind Creator for a favoured creature, the amplest conceivable provision for a being of the most capacious and various desires. The surface of the earth is strewn with flowers; the path of years is paved and planted with enjoyments. Every sort of beauty has been lavished on our allotted home; beauties to enrapture every sense, beauties to satisfy every taste. Forms the noblest and the loveliest, colours the most gorgeous and the most delicate, odours the sweetest and the subtlest, harmonies the most soothing and the most stirring; the sunny glades of the day, the pale Elysian grace of moonlight, the lake, the mountain, the primeval forest, and the boundless ocean;

silent pinnacles of aged snow in one hemisphere, the marvels of tropical luxuriance in another; the serenity of sunsets; the sublimity of storms; in short, *everything* is bestowed in boundless profusion on the scene of our present existence. *We can conceive or desire nothing more exquisite or perfect than what is around us every hour.* And our perceptions are so framed as to be consciously alive to all. The provision made for our sensuous enjoyment is in overflowing abundance; so is that for the other elements of our complex nature. Who that has revelled in the opening ecstasies of a young imagination, or the rich marvels of the world of thought, does not confess that the intelligence has been dowered at least with as profuse a beneficence as the senses! Who that has truly tasted and *fathomed* human love, in its dawning and its crowning joys, has not thanked God for a felicity which indeed "passeth understanding"! If [he goes on to say] we had set our fancy to picture a Creator occupied solely in devising for children, whom He loved, we could not conceive one single element of bliss which is not here. We might retrench casualties; we might superadd duration and extension; we might make that which is partial, occasional, and transient, universal and enduring; but we need not, and we could not, introduce one new ingredient of joy.'*

This is certainly a very highly coloured and beautiful picture of our present state, and one (which many of us, perhaps, will think) scarcely borne out by our daily experience. Still, it will serve our purpose, if we remember, while gazing at it, that even if it were a perfect reflection of the realities of this life, it would no more image forth the immeasurably greater delights of Heaven than the midday sun, painted by some poor earthly artist upon canvas, can image forth the actual fiery orb which God Himself has set in the arching heavens above.

Spiritual writers sometimes invite us, when making our meditation on Heaven, to recall to mind the very happiest moment of our present existence—that moment which comes as a rule to most men once during the course ot their lives—a moment of quite exceptional

* *Vide* 'Enigmas of Life,' by W. R. Greg, pp. 185, 186.

joy, and perfect peace, when earth seems all smiles, and the heavens all love, and our whole being is flooded with pure sunshine, and we seem to have been accorded just a passing taste of perfect bliss, as though a single drop from the boundless ocean of celestial delights enjoyed by the Blessed had fallen between our lips, and had intoxicated us with rapturous delight. Take such a moment, they tell us, and intensify that experience a hundred thousand fold, and then extend it, in imagination, throughout eternity, and then reflect that the celestial joys, actually filling the hearts of the Blessed at this moment, are incomparably greater and more intense.

In examining the risen body, we must note two distinct things. The first is its natural perfection; and the second is the added supernatural perfection which is conferred through the special properties or attributes, which it receives from God, to render it no longer a hindrance, but a fit and helpful companion of the glorified soul. In so far as the first is concerned, let us bear in mind that the risen body will possess every limb and organ, and every sense and power which a fully developed and healthy body now possesses,* but with this difference, that each organ will be absolutely perfect and thoroughly sound and healthy. As the five senses are now the five great means by which man puts himself in communication with the external world around him, so, too, through these same five senses, though greatly perfected, will he, in his glorified state, put himself in relation with the sources of delight around him in Paradise.

All theologians teach that the risen body retains its five organs of sense. Some think that these senses may even be added to, and that others, of which we can, of course, form no conception whatsoever, may also be given us: and all these senses will have full play, and be gratified to the uttermost. The inspired writer, referring to our present imperfect state, observes here that 'the eye is

* 'Manebit diversitas sexus; haec enim est naturalis; et quod naturae est quam ipse fecit, non mutabit Deus; sed reparabit.' . . . 'Si in statu innocentiae nuditatem non erubescebant primi parentes, quia ab eo aberat libido incentiva; haec multo magis aberit a statu gloriae.'—'Wirceburgensis,' v. 16.

not filled with seeing, neither is the ear filled with hearing' (Eccles. i. 8). But in Heaven, not only the eye and the ear, but every sense will be filled, and completely satisfied. We may each of us exclaim, with holy David: 'I shall be satisfied, when Thy glory shall appear' (Ps. xvi. 15). I—that is to say, *my whole being*, therefore my senses as well as my soul—will be satisfied, when God manifests His glory in His heavenly kingdom. In short, not only the powers of the soul, but the senses of the body also, will be fully gratified and will overflow with unspeakable pleasure. We may gather as much from the very nature and character of God. He is infinitely good in Himself. He is immeasurably more generous and lavish in rewarding than in punishing; infinitely more disposed to increase the joys of the elect than to multiply the sorrows of the lost. If, then, every sense of the damned will be tormented, and more especially those in which they have chiefly offended, it must surely follow that, in the case of the elect, every sense will be most abundantly gratified, and more especially those which have been religiously mortified and restrained. There are, indeed, certain sources of earthly pleasure, of a sensual kind, which St. Paul tells us 'should not so much as be named among Christians' (Ephes. v. 3), but to which men are much addicted in this world. *Such* pleasures, of course, cannot have any possible place in Heaven, because they are impure and unbecoming. But, though earthly pleasures of that nature are wholly unthinkable among the Blessed, yet the repression and the mortification of such by the faithful followers of Christ, while on earth, will be rewarded by other pleasures not only absolutely pure, but immeasurably more delectable and satisfying, though utterly beyond our present power to conceive.*

* 'Certum est beatorum corpora non fore sensibus destituta, sed perfectissime instructa, cum perfectissimis organis et spiritibus ad usum eorum opportunis; ac proinde habitura sensuum usum, eumque perfectissimum. Et sane frustra resumeretur corpus, si non foret ibi sensuum usus et oblectatio; cum corpus humanum non sit necessarium aut utile animae nisi propter sensuum usum. Neque etiam defutura sunt objecta quae percipiantur et oblectent sensus. Confirmatur *primo*, quia singuli sensus capaces sunt summae cujusdam perfectionis sui ordinis, quae singulorum est beatitudo, et vita beata, quam facile et sine incommodo vel indecoro possunt in patria habere; cur ergo reipsa non

Padre B. Rogacci, S.J., writing of the Blessed, says: 'Each of their senses will enjoy as much pleasure as it can desire.' Then, after speaking in turn of the delights of sight, hearing, taste, and smell, he goes on to say:

'And, lastly, the sense of touch, with a healthy vigour and ethereal keenness, will be diffused through all the organs of the body, causing it to feel a pleasure, free indeed from the excitement and weariness of sensual pleasures, but, as to the degree of gratification, *far greater than all of them. . . .* For their bodies will have been formed by God Himself with a workmanship miraculously exquisite, and surpassing all the works of nature, *for no other end but that of perfect and infinite enjoyment.* From this it may be gathered what a mere nothing, when con-

---

habeant? Confirmatur *secundo*, quia anima non solum est rationalis, sed etiam sensitiva; et in utraque parte capax est oblectationum, et vitae cujusdam beatae; ergo non solum in parte rationali beari debet (quod fiet per visionem et fruitionem Dei), sed etiam in parte sentiente, quod fiet perceptione praestantissimorum objectorum sensibilium, singulis sensibus accommodatorum.'—L. Lessius, 'De Summo Bono,' chap. viii., p. 539.

trasted with this incomparable felicity, are both the gratifications with which sinners indulge their flesh and the mortifications with which the Saints afflict it; and that the man who has the most love for his body is he who, by chastising it during this short life, merits for it so happy a state in eternity.'

Referring to man's life in this world, it has often been remarked that God, in His wisdom, has annexed certain pleasures to actions which, according to the divine plan, have to be performed, and which would otherwise run the risk of being neglected. We will take two examples, though they might be considerably added to. In the first place, it is required that man should preserve his natural life; as a consequence, he must eat and drink at pretty frequent intervals. This is certainly a duty which would often be neglected if it involved nothing but trouble and nausea. So, to render the duty easy and of universal acceptance, God has attached a certain pleasure to the process of eating and drinking, and has given to both food and drink a distinct savour and a relish which make them acceptable to the ordinary man, so that, speaking generally, the duty of self-preservation becomes not only easy, but unmistakably agreeable. But, further, not only has the individual to be preserved, but the race, as a whole, has to be perpetuated and propagated. So here, likewise, God has thought fit to connect certain very special pleasures with the process. Scarcely any man or woman would be found ready and willing to undertake the arduous duties and the grave responsibilities of parentage were there no strong incentives to draw the sexes together, and to make marriage, for the great bulk of mankind, really attractive and desirable.

But, as the duties connected with this state of life are exceptionally onerous and troublesome, God has annexed to it many exceptionally great attractions. In fact, He has made the path of duty, in this case, so exceedingly pleasant and attractive that there never has been any difficulty whatever on the part of His creatures to fulfil the command to 'increase and to multiply, and to fill the earth' (Gen. i. 28). Perhaps it may even be allowed that God has associated with this state of marriage some of the highest and most intense natural delights of which man is capable in this world.

But, in these and in all other similar instances, these natural pleasures are bestowed in order to aid in the carrying out of certain definite and important purposes. They constitute the 'oil of joy' (*darem eis oleum gaudii pro luctu*) of which Isaias speaks (lxi. 3), the oil which makes the machinery run smoothly and easily. As an earthly father will coat a bitter pill with honey to render it sweet and palatable and readily swallowed by his fastidious little children, so our heavenly Father condescends to coat with a specially sweet honey many of the vital actions which men are called upon to perform on earth, which otherwise would be found far too burdensome and intolerable to be endured. But the point to be insisted upon is, that though we are helped in this way to do our duty, yet the present life is not exactly intended to be a period of unclouded pleasure and tranquil happiness, whereas our future life is most certainly designed to be of that character. Hence, if God provides certain pleasures and joys, for the purpose of smoothing the rough ways of earth, and of alleviating the burdens of life here, He will certainly provide hereafter pleasures and joys immeasurably more ravishing and fascinating than the most favoured has ever experienced, or even dreamed of, in this life of trial and chastisement. If, indeed, it be true that the worst punishments of this world are small and contemptible as compared with those of the next, it is no less certain that the pleasures and the delights of this world are also quite as poor and contemptible as compared with the pleasures and the delights of the next. We must bear in mind that the five senses of the human body are not mere accidental ornaments, which may be dispensed with in another life. They are *essential to the integrity of its nature.* Now, as glory does not destroy the nature of the body, but, on the contrary, perfects it, it follows that all the Blessed must rise with their five senses, in full perfection. Further, as their perfection consists in their activity, and in their power to receive impressions from external objects, and to convey them to the soul, it is perfectly clear that the senses must remain active in

Heaven, and be provided with suitable objects to act upon.

This is the teaching of the Angelic Doctor, who lays it down that 'Potentia conjuncta actui suo perfectior est quam non conjuncta; sed humana natura erit in beatis in maxima perfectione; ergo erunt ibi *omnes sensus in suo actu.* Praeterea, vicinius se habent ad animam potentiae sensitivae, quam corpus; sed corpus praemiabitur vel punietur propter merita vel demerita animae; ergo et *omnes sensus praemiabuntur* in beatis, et punientur in malis, secundum delectationem et dolorem vel tristitiam, quae in operatione sensus consistunt.'* Hence, we have quite as much reason to dwell with complacency on the delights of the glorified senses of the just, when we are meditating on Heaven, as we have to dwell with horror and terror on the excruciating torments of the senses, in the reprobate, when contemplating the infernal regions. The joys of the one are every bit as real as the agonies of the other, and quite as well calculated to move and influence our will.

In conclusion, we may point out that though man will possess a body in Heaven,

* Supplement, Question LXXXII., Article 4.

as well as a soul, yet he will not in any way be hampered or impeded by it, but will enjoy the self-same liberty of movement and freedom of action as the Angels themselves. In fact, man will possess something over and above what the Angels possess, and therefore (in a certain sense) will be even more privileged and happier than they; for, while fully sharing with the Angels their gifts of agility, subtlety, brightness, and impassibility, and so forth, he will, *in addition to all these,* possess a perfectly mobile body, as well as his five corporal senses, each of which will procure for him innumerable pleasures and delights, of which a pure spirit, such as an Angel, can have no actual experience. Hence, as theologians observe, 'Though man's happiness may not be greater than that of an Angel *intensively,* it will be greater *extensively.*'*

* 'Habebit homo gloriam corporis, et multiplices in corpore et per corporis sensus voluptates, quibus Angeli carent. Unde, homo erit beatior extensive; quia ejus beatitudo non continebit se in anima, sed effundet se in corpus, juxta sententiam St. Augustini (Epis. 56): "Tam potenti natura Deus fecit animam, ut ex ejus plenissima beatitudine, quae in fine temporum sanctis promittitur, redundet etiam in inferiorem naturam, quod est corpus." '—L. Lessius, 'De Summo Bono,' p. 422.

# CHAPTER III

## SUPERNATURAL KNOWLEDGE

I am glad that I am going;
What a strange and sweet delight,
Is thro' all my being flowing
When I know that, sure, to-night
I will pass from earth and meet Him,
Whom I loved thro' all the years,
Who will crown me when I greet Him,
And will kiss away my tears.

FATHER RYAN.

TO a soul rejoicing in Heaven, the body will be a veritable storehouse of exquisite delights. Even the greatest saints, who have crucified their flesh in this life, speak of it in wonder and admiration, as a source of pleasures untold and wholly inexpressible. As our own experience has, no doubt, taught us, there are many internal organs and muscles and nerves functioning within our mortal frame of whose very existence we are scarcely aware, until they get out of order, and torment us with racking pains. But, in the next life, each and every one of these organs and nerves will be recognized, not, indeed, by the pains they cause, but by reason of the exquisite pleasures to which they give rise. St. Anselm writes: 'In the heavenly courts everything will unite in proclaiming the glory of God. For not only the souls, but the bodies of the Just also, and all their parts and organs, will rejoice in the presence of their Creator.' The Saint even goes so far as to enumerate the chief of these organs.* 'Eyes, ears, nose, mouth, hand, throat, heart, liver, lungs, bones, etc.,' he writes, 'will be filled with such sweetness and delectation that the whole man may truly be said to drink of the torrent of delights, and to be, as it were, inebriated with the abundance of God's house.'

Other saints and holy men express themselves in a similar manner. Thus, after describing some of the most atrocious and

* 'Oculi, aures, nares, os, manus, guttur, cor, jecur, pulmo, ossa, medullae, et cuncta singillatim membra eorum in communi, tam mirabili delectationis et dulcedinis sensu replebuntur ut vere totus homo torrente voluptatis Dei potetur, et ab ubertate domus ejus inebrietur.'—*Vide* 'Lib. De Similitud.,' cap. 57.

excruciating torments of the martyrs, Fra Ermenegildo da Chitignano, M.R., observes as follows: 'Nevertheless, even the very worst of these agonies bears no sort of proportion to the very least of the delights that the Just will enjoy, in their risen bodies.' For 'such torments as the martyrs endured,' he goes on to observe, 'are torments inflicted by man, and, even when most prolonged, are soon over, whereas all the delights which the Blessed will enjoy, even in their bodies, in Heaven, are effected by the infinite power and munificence of God Himself, and are eternal. Hence,' he continues, 'St. Paul may well assure the Romans that the sufferings of this time are not worthy to be compared with the glory to come, which shall be revealed in us' (Rom. viii. 18).

Although worldly-minded men attach an altogether exaggerated importance to sensual pleasures, and will shamefully sacrifice God and Heaven and all else of value for the sake of a passing act of self-indulgence, yet such earthly pleasures do not merit even the name of pleasures at all when compared with the pleasures of the life to come. If, indeed, we could actually experience even the very least and lowest of the corporal pleasures experienced by the Blessed in their bright Home above, it would be enough, and more than enough, to give us a distaste for all such pleasures as we know of, on earth; just as the listening to a chorus of exquisite music rendered by some full and perfect orchestra would extinguish any delight we might otherwise feel in listening to the same score, painfully scratched out by an amateur on a badly tuned fiddle.

We have spoken of the pleasures of the senses because they are more tangible and make a more ready appeal to us than those which are spiritual. In fact, we are so dependent upon the senses in this life, and are so constantly employing them, that we find it far more easy to appreciate them than things which are more abstract. But this renders it all the more essential for us to realize that, after all, the body, even the risen and glorified body, must be regarded as a poor and unworthy object so soon as it is contrasted with the soul. If, therefore, the senses of the body can procure us such immense delights, there is no doubt but that the powers and faculties of the glorified soul will open out to us joys and delights unspeakably and inconceivably greater. Of these faculties the chief are the intellect and the will. The will has to do with love and the affections, and the intellect has to do with truth and knowledge. Let us consider the intellect first. Every man can form some idea of the pleasures derived from study and the exercise of the understanding. We may all exclaim:

> Oh for a book and a shadie nook,
>   Eyther in doore or out;
> With the green leaves whispering overhead,
>   Or the streete cryes all about.
> Where I maie reade all at my ease,
>   Both of the newe and olde;
> For a jolly goode booke whereon to looke
>   Is better to me than golde.
>
> (*Old English Song.*)

We are all aware that, even in this world, great numbers find their happiness in the pursuit of Truth, in its myriad forms. Indeed, Truth possesses such a fascination in itself that the appetite for it only increases by indulgence. So that it may be truly asserted that the more men know, the keener becomes their desire to extend their knowledge still further, and the more ravenous grows their appetite. Yet, in spite of this, it must be confessed that all the knowledge that the most famous and diligent student ever acquired in this life is simply nothing as compared to the sum of knowledge possessed by the very least of the Blessed. So long as we are in this world we are constantly formulating questions to which we know no satisfactory answer can be given. Experience must have long since convinced us that on a vast number of interesting subjects we must content ourselves to remain ignorant. Even that great genius Sir Isaac Newton, speaking on this subject, said: 'I do not know what I may appear to the world, but to myself I seem to have been only like a boy playing on the sea-shore, and diverting myself in, now and then, finding a smoother pebble or a prettier shell than ordinary, whilst the vast ocean of truth lay all undiscovered before me.' The remarks made by the late Marquis of Salisbury in his address on Evolution (1894) are also to the point: 'We live,' he said, 'in a small bright oasis of knowledge, surrounded on all sides by a vast unexplored region of impenetrable mystery. From age to age the strenuous labour of successive generations wins a small strip from the desert, and pushes forward the boundary of knowledge.' But, notwithstanding all our efforts, the known, as compared to the unknown, still remains less than a single grain of sand compared to an immense mountain range.

To assist us in realizing our ignorance, let us pay an imaginary visit to the British Museum, and consider the prodigious sum of human knowledge that is now stored up within its walls. In its vast Library, the great shelves laden with books are so numerous that we are told that if they were laid together, end to end, they would extend to a distance of over forty-six miles. Let us take up our position in the midst of these endless series of book-cases, surrounded by millions of volumes, on every side. Almost every book that has ever been published on Theology, Philosophy, History, Science, Literature, Biology, Geology, Mathematics, and the rest is to be found there. Suppose now it were possible to (as it were) melt down all the knowledge contained in all these volumes, and to pour it, without spilling a drop, into the head of a single individual such-wise that he might have the whole (as we may say) 'at his beck and call.' What a perfect marvel of learning he would be! The whole world would acknowledge him to be by far, not only the greatest philosopher that had ever lived, but the greatest historian, and the greatest scientist, and so on as regards every other branch of learning. He would contain within his own single mind the learning of all those who have written. He would be regarded as a walking encyclopædia; yea, the very quintessence of wisdom, such as it would be difficult to describe. Yet, even he would be, in reality, uninformed and ignorant, so soon as he is compared with the very least and last of the inhabitants of Heaven.

Merely for the sake of argument we have supposed the impossible. We have supposed that all the knowledge stored up in the five or six millions of books, pamphlets, and manuscripts lying in the British Museum to be miraculously transferred to the brain of one single individual. But even so, what, after all, would it amount to? The learned works on History, Science, Literature, and the rest may be countless in number, but they all, without exception, deal *only with this one tiny and insignificant earth and its inhabitants*, and with what may be seen from its surface (*e.g.*, Astronomy).

Man has indeed been studying, and investigating, and examining, and scrutinizing the earth ever since he was placed upon it. But how very little he knows *even of the one small planet on which he dwells!* The surface of the earth he has but scratched. Into its bowels he has never penetrated, nor has he ever explored the vast caves and hidden depths of the ocean. There are numberless objects in the mineral, vegetable, and animal kingdoms of which he knows next to nothing. But even supposing he knew all that there is to be known of this earth, it would mean exceedingly little. It would mean simply that he had become acquainted with one of the smallest and most insignificant of the planets, floating, like a microscopic grain of dust, amid a vast and wholly incalculable multitude of immensely greater worlds. All around millions upon millions of orbs are revolving of which he knows little more than the bare fact of their existence. Astronomers inform us that Mr. Franklin Adams recently photographed the whole sky, on two hundred and six plates, containing altogether fifty-five million stars. And it is computed, from the sequence of the numbers for different magnitudes, that there cannot be less than a thousand million whose light has already reached the earth, and that probably there are over two thousand millions scattered through space.

Furthermore, these stars or suns are, for the most part, immensely bigger than the earth. We may form some idea of the size of our own sun by what we have learned lately of a group of spots, which stretched from near the centre of the sun almost half-way to the western or right-hand limb, and extended for at least 300,000 miles in length. The total area occupied by the group was probably not less (it is said) than 4,000,000,000 square miles. The sun is so far away that we cannot see any spot with the naked eye that contains less than 500,000,000 square miles, but there was one in this group which we are assured contained more than 700,000,000 square miles, and which might have been observed through a thickly smoked glass, even without telescopic assistance. Now, it must be remembered that, in spite of its many hundreds of millions of miles, our sun is but a single star, and (when compared to others) of but medium size. It is merely its proximity that invests it with the value and importance which we attach to it. Some of the larger suns are, not millions only, but billions of times vaster than the earth. Thus, to give a single instance: astronomers point to a star, in the constellation of Orion, Alpha Orionis, known by the name of Betelgeuse, which is billions of times the bulk of the world which we inhabit. This startling fact will be brought more vividly before our mind if we reflect that the diameter of the earth is somewhat over eight thousand miles, and that the diameter of the sun itself is only something over eight hundred thousand miles, whereas the diameter of Betelgeuse is said to be no less than 237,000,000 miles. It must, therefore, reduce our sun, *by comparison,* to a very insignificant star indeed. The well-known astronomer Rev. A. L. Cortie, S.J., informs me that 'with an approximate distance of 180 light years, the star is 237,000,000 miles in diameter. It is, therefore, more than 270 times the diameter of our sun, and 21,000,000 times its volume.'

When we consider, further, that many of these colossal suns are attended by numbers of planets circulating round them, we shall the more easily realize that any knowledge we may possess of the earth will be but *the knowledge of one small and very unimportant grain of dust,* floating amid countless thousands of vaster orbs surrounding it, for billions upon billions of miles, in every direction.

Nor must it be forgotten that even such poor and fragmentary knowledge of the heavens as the ablest astronomers possess is acquired only by dint of patient study, prolonged and severe application, and many sleepless nights of careful watching, whereas the knowledge of the Blessed is not only full and perfect, but it is obtained without trouble or fatigue. By means of the light of glory, they will be able to read the infinite book of Nature, through and through, with the utmost ease and accuracy, and will be able to contemplate and examine all the most marvellous wonders of the visible universe, stretching out to untold distances upon every side. 'Ad statum Beatorum pertinet, res naturales perfecte cognoscere' ('Wirceburgensis,' tom. v., p. 19).

We in this world may compare ourselves to men locked up, during a pitch dark night, in a great museum. So circumstanced, we should know practically nothing of the nature, and the character, and the beauty of the various objects around us. Perhaps by passing our hands over some, and feeling them carefully, we might at last gain some faint and hazy knowledge of a few of the simplest. But so soon as ever the sun rises in the heavens, and illuminates the whole scene, we should distinguish each object, realize its form and colour and construction, and, in short, learn *more at a single glance* than we could have learned during the entire night of fruitless endeavour. This is a good illustration, for theologians tell us that 'Lumen gloriae praestat respectu intellectus beati, quod lumen corporale respectu oculorum' ('Wirceburgensis,' v., p. 5).

So, in a somewhat similar way, during the night of this present life, we may grope about in the dark, and with immense difficulty gain some imperfect acquaintance with the universe around us. But it is only when the bright Sun of Justice arises in all His might—*i.e.*, only when God withdraws the veil that hides Him from us—that the darkness of our present ignorance vanishes in His glorious light, and the full beauty and splendour of the Creation is revealed. 'For then the Lord Himself shall be for an everlasting light' (Isa. lx. 19). And we shall cry out as we contemplate the ravishing scene, 'Thou art worthy, O Lord our God, to receive glory and honour and power; because Thou hast created all things; and for Thy will they were and have been created' (Apoc. iv. 11).

The objects of celestial knowledge will be not only most numerous, but also most varied. The lowest will be the material creation, which we shall see stretching out before us, in all directions, and to endless distances.

With minds filled with wonder at the Divine power and wisdom, we shall contemplate the marvels of earth, sun, and moon, and of the myriads upon myriads of gleaming stars, scattered with the most lavish profusion over the whole firmament of heaven. We shall learn all the laws that govern the formation, the development, and the movements of these celestial bodies, their intricate relationship to one another, and all the secrets of their complicated, though orderly and harmonious, flight through the unmeasured realms of space. Indeed, the whole system upon which the sideral universe has been built up, as well as its gradual growth and development and general history, will be taken in at a glance.

With the same ease we shall also acquaint ourselves with the entire history of the animal creation, with its infinite variety of genera and species, as well as with the habits, nature, characteristics, and peculiarities and endowments and strange instincts and modes of life of each. But what is more interesting—the story of the human race, from Adam to the last man—will be unfolded to us, together with all the events associated with its multiplication and extension all over the world, its gradual civilization, the rise of all the arts and sciences, the inventions, discoveries, and improvements; as also its struggles, conflicts, dangers, and difficulties, and the rest.*

Perhaps the most intensely interesting object of contemplation, to the glorified race, in this connection, will be that of the hitherto hidden action of Divine Providence in the affairs of man, and its marvellous intervention in the most critical moments, and in the most momentous crises of life. It will be given to us to learn, with the utmost accuracy, the career of each individual, the struggles that went on within his soul between grace and nature, inclination and duty, and between

* 'Non videri dubitandum, quin beati vi illius luminis possint distincte et clare intueri, quidquid intra complexum mundi ac totius hujus universi continetur. Sicut enim totum Deum clare vident, ita etiam totum opus Dei, quod intra Deum et infra Deum est, et intra et supra quod ipse Deus est, intueri debent; cum primarius finis operis hujus sit, ut divina majestas ejusque potentia, sapientia, benignitas, sanctitas, misericordia, justitia, providentia in eo resplendeat Angelorum et hominum mentibus, et ipsa ex eo laudetur et benedicatur.' —Lessius, l. ii., chap. x., p. 204.

the human and the Divine Will, as well as all his hidden trials and temptations.

St. Paul, in his First Epistle to the Corinthians (iv. 5), warns us not to judge 'until the Lord come, *who both will bring to light the hidden things of darkness, and will make manifest the counsels of the hearts.*' From this and similar texts, commentators infer that we shall not only see God, but that in God we shall see, with the utmost clearness, the entire universe, together with all its parts, and everything concerning each part. So that there will be no object, whether person or thing, whether material or spiritual, which shall not be perfectly known and understood. In fact, created persons and things will be known in two distinct ways: firstly, '*cognitione matutina,*' as theologians express it, and, secondly, '*cognitione vespertina*'—that is to say, firstly, in their cause, which is God, and, secondly, in themselves. In both these ways the vast creation, with every conceivable object it contains, will be rendered distinct and clear to the contemplating mind, even 'the hidden things of darkness,' and the secret 'counsels of the hearts.'

We shall know all that the glorious saints and martyrs have suffered and endured in their noble efforts to win the crown of immortal glory. We shall be filled with wonder and admiration at the thousand unsuspected and loving ways in which God has protected them, watched over them, and brought them strength and courage in their hour of need. We shall marvel at the dangers they have run, the difficulties they have overcome, and all the temptations and wiles of the devil, which they have so bravely resisted and triumphed over, by means of the constant and ever vigilant providence of God.

A greater delight still will flow into our souls, from the knowledge given us of God's direct action upon the world, such as His institution of the infallible Church; the invention of the seven great Sacraments, with all the special graces and supernatural effects that they produce. The wonders of the Incarnation; the twofold natures united in the one adorable Person; the numerous mysteries contained in the eucharistic presence of Christ in the Blessed Sacrament; the presence of His divinity and His humanity, with all the attributes of His glorified soul and body, in every tiny particle of the consecrated Host, will all be made manifest. To these we may add all the innumerable mysteries in connection with the justification and election and glorification of innumerable souls.

From a knowledge of God's dealings with men upon earth, we shall rise to the contemplation of the still greater wonders which He has wrought in Heaven. Each of the glorious spirits who stand before the 'great white Throne of God' will furnish us with an object worthy of our most earnest and loving contemplation. Every separate individual of each of the nine choirs will fill us with profound and glowing wonder and admiration and delight as we gaze upon him. If, indeed, we accept the teaching of the Angelic Doctor on the point, and regard each member of the angelic host as a distinct species, it must be admitted that each one will exhibit before our amazed eyes a wholly new and perfectly unique world of beauty, glory, splendour, and loveliness. From these and from countless other equally exquisite creations of God, we shall rise to what is infinitely more admirable still—namely, to the contemplation of God Himself. 'God is wonderful in all His works,' says the Psalmist. 'Great and wonderful are Thy works, O Lord God Almighty; and just and true are Thy ways, O King of ages,' exclaims St. John (Apoc. xv. 3). But even these most sublime and fascinating objects of contemplation will not wholly satisfy us, nor fill our minds. They will rather inflame them with a yet more burning thirst to know something of an object infinitely greater still, infinitely more beautiful and perfect and of inexhaustible splendour. For having feasted the eyes of our soul on the foremost and most transcendent works of God *ad extra*, we shall be consumed with an insatiable longing to gaze upon the infinite Author of all these wonders, viewed *in His own nature*. We may find endless delights in studying His creatures, but we cannot be wholly content till He shows Himself. 'We shall be satisfied when His glory shall appear,' but not before.

Though God's attributes are all absolutely one, and in themselves indistinguishable, as they exist in the Divine essence, yet, as our finite minds conceive them, they are innumerable. Each attribute and perfection is so full, so profound, so measureless, and so inconceivably rich, that no created mind, whether of man or angel, can ever sound one of them to its bottomless depths. Though God will undoubtedly admit us to His unveiled presence, and though we shall see Him 'as He is,' yet our knowledge will not and cannot be really adequate. The finite can never contain the Infinite. However perfectly the Blessed may know God's Divine perfections, there will always remain infinitely more to learn. Though eternity is long, yet even eternity itself will not be long enough for even the keenest intelligence among the Cherubim or Seraphim to measure the height and the depth and the length and the breadth of the uncreated and eternal God. If we are among the Blessed, we shall contemplate Him for ever; and for ever we shall continue to discover new beauties, and fresh wonders, and undreamed-of splendours, and unimagined excellences—yet a period will never come when we shall be able to exclaim: Now my knowledge is full and complete, and nothing more remains to be discovered.*

In the myriads of saints and angels we contemplate the dazzling beauty with which God has clothed them, and our whole being thrills at the sight. But now we are permitted actually to feast our eyes upon that which is infinitely greater, and which it is impossible for us to find in any creature whatsoever, because it is absolutely incommunicable—we mean the eternal, uncreated, and infinite beauty of God Himself. Each attribute, each perfection, each excellence, will stir and thrill our whole being to its uttermost capacity. Each, even taken singly, would be more than enough, not only to satisfy, but to fill to overflowing and to flood our whole being with rapturous delight, and to hold us enthralled for ever and ever.

* The great St. Bonaventure reminds us: 'Non solum non cor hominis viatoris, sed, nec etiam comprehensoris, aut alicujus angeli potest aut poterit illud bonum infinitum et gaudium nobis paratum et oblatum *comprehendere.*'—'Breviloquium,' Pars vii. 7, p. 667.

And Lessius writes: 'Nullus intellectus creatus potest essentiam divinam comprehendere, sed quantumvis perfecte illam videat, haec tamen visio *in infinitum a comprehensione distat.*'—L. ii., c. x., p. 183.

What, then, can we say will be the effect of feasting our eyes, not on one attribute only, but upon all united! Here not words only, but thought itself fails us. Yet such is our destiny and the reward awaiting us. A reward which will most certainly be ours shortly, if only we bring our ship safely into port, and wreck not our 'earthen vessels' (2 Cor. iv. 7) by the commission of sin.

There are many subjects of investigation in this world which have little, if any, beauty to recommend them. Yet even these men are found to study and to inquire into, either from a spirit of curiosity or for profit, or out of pure love of discovery. But where the object is itself full of beauty and loveliness, every increase of knowledge and every step forward is not only an increase of knowledge, but is also *an increase of joy and delight.* When, for example, a discoverer approaches for the first time some tropical land of exceptional luxuriousness and beauty, and directs his ship up one of its winding rivers into the very heart of the country, he will receive successive new impressions of delight at each stage of the journey. Each fresh mile traversed, each fresh bend in the river, will bring him in view of new and unfamiliar fruits and flowers, birds and beasts, as well as of fairy glens and enchanting valleys, and fruitful fields and meadows.

Now, if this be true of even the created and material and limited beauty of the physical world, who will describe the constantly fresh impressions of delight and rapture received by a soul in glory, as it passes on, from the contemplation of one beauty to another, in the exhaustless and infinite being of God; a beauty so rare, so unique and unapproachable, so immeasurable and fecund, so absolutely perfect, and—until actually seen—so unimaginable and inconceivable!

But no language can convey any adequate picture of such happiness. It must be experienced to be understood, and actually enjoyed before it can be appreciated. Even those very few saints who have been favoured during life with some momentary glimpses of such a beatific vision can only declare with St. Paul, that 'it is not granted to man to utter' the wonders which they experienced. Let us, then, consider well these truths, and try to possess ourselves in patience, until the great day of Eternity dawns, and the shadows depart, and the glorious Sun of Justice rises, in all its unparalleled brightness and splendour, never to set again, but to continue to enchant and to rejoice us all with its dazzling and life-giving presence, for ever and ever, in our heavenly Home. Death will soon throw open the golden gates for us; so let us hasten to fit ourselves more and more perfectly for the great summons: 'Enter into the joy of the Lord.'

## CHAPTER IV

## LOVE IS HEAVEN; AND HEAVEN IS LOVE

E'en such is Time, that takes in trust
Our youth, our joys, our all we have,
And pays us but with earth and dust;
Who in the dark and silent grave,
When we have wandered all our ways,
Shuts up the story of our days;
*But from this earth, this grave, this dust,*
*My God shall raise me up, I trust.*

(*Written by Sir Walter Raleigh just before his execution,* 1618.)

OF all the many joys that inflame man's sensitive heart, by far the greatest and the intensest, as well as the most universally appreciated and esteemed, are the joys which arise from the exercise of love. What the sun is to the material world, that love is to the social world. Love brings warmth into the most desolate and desponding heart; it cheers, brightens, and consoles the most afflicted and lonely life, and bestows new strength and power and energy upon the sorrowing and the depressed. In short, it registers the very highest watermark of earthly happiness. As Thomas Moore truly says:

> New hopes may rise, and days may come
> Of milder, calmer beam,
> But there's nothing half so sweet in life
> As Love's young dream.

Love is the very soul of music, of poetry, and of romance. It forms the unvarying theme of every novelist, playwright, and *raconteur*. For 'the old, old story,' though ever old, is ever new; and even though related over and over again, in a thousand different ways, it never palls nor tires. Love, indeed, rules and reigns triumphantly in every heart, if once it can effect an entrance therein:

> Love rules the court, the camp, the grove,
> And men below and saints above:
> For love is heaven, and heaven is love.

And, as love is the greatest source of joy on earth, so is it the greatest source of joy in Heaven. 'Now there remain faith, hope, and love, these three; but the greatest of these is love' (1 Cor. xiii. 13). Although faith and hope attend us, as faithful companions, to the very gates of Paradise, there they bid us an eternal farewell. Whereas love, on the contrary, enters in exultantly, and will abide with us and delight us for ever and ever, so long as God is God.

In that thrice happy region God's love will be more to us than any of His other Divine perfections. Hence it is not surprising that the Holy Scriptures lay such stress on that particular attribute. Although God is Wisdom, and Power, and Justice, and all else, yet the inspired Book does not say so, in explicit terms. But it does declare, in the most emphatic manner, '*Deus charitas est*'—'*God is* LOVE' (1 John iv. 8), and furthermore, it teaches us that 'he that abideth in charity, abideth in God and God in him' (1 John iv. 7). Hence charity unites us immediately with God. In Heaven, the impelling force which inspires and kindles our love is God's infinite beauty and perfections, which shall be clearly exhibited to the elect. Now we may observe here that it is a well-recognized fact, proved by experience, that our nature is so formed by God as to receive a special pleasure and delight from the contemplation of any object which is perfect in its kind and of great beauty. Consider, for instance, the very lowest form of beauty—namely, material beauty, let us say the beauty of the human form. Though this is the very least *kind* of beauty, yet it is the highest *of its kind*, and will exercise a most remarkable power over every beholder. In fact, a perfect specimen of a fully developed human being, as history proves by a thousand instances, possesses an almost incredible power of attracting to itself the hearts of those who behold it, even though they may be most wise and powerful. Experience proves that often the mere sight of one surpassingly fair and lovely will throw a spell over all beholders, and in a manner, bewitch and enchant them, owing to the pleasure and delight that it excites. Nor is it necessary to have recourse to profane history for examples of this undoubted fact. The Holy Scriptures abound with illustrations. Witness such examples as we find in the histories of Samson, Solomon, and of Holofernes and of numberless others.

When Judith was on her way to the camp

of Holofernes, she was at first stopped by the watchmen of the Assyrians; but 'when they beheld her face their eyes were amazed, for they wondered exceedingly at her beauty' (Judith x. 14). And, instead of stopping her, 'they brought her to the tent of Holofernes, and when she was come into his presence, forthwith Holofernes was likewise caught by his eyes' (x. 17). The very rareness of her beauty gave her an astounding victory, and, in fact, indirectly, enabled her to free her people from the dreaded power of the Assyrians. Esther is another case in point. Her marvellous beauty at once won over the king. Although it was well known that 'anyone who dared to enter into the king's inner court without being summoned was *immediately to be put to death,*' yet Esther's extraordinary loveliness enabled her successfully to run the risk. By reason of her great attractions she was able to soften the heart of the king, and so to escape this terrible fate. For, 'when he saw Esther, she pleased his eyes.' And so far from ordering her 'to be put to death immediately, and without delay' (Esther iv. 11), as the law demanded, he received her most graciously, saying, 'What wilt thou? What is thy request? If thou shouldst even ask one half of the kingdom, it shall be given to thee' (v. 3).

Even the great and wise Solomon could not resist the bewitching influence of beauty. The beautiful daughters of Moab, and of Ammon, and of Edom, and of Sidon, and of the Hethites (3 Kings xi. 1) threw such a spell over him, and so captivated his heart, that 'his mind was turned away from the Lord, the God of Israel' (3 Kings xi. 9), and his only thought was to give them pleasure.

Thus, it is clearly seen that even mere physical beauty, when it is very exceptional, exercises an extraordinary power, and captivates all beholders. The usual effect is to give joy and gladness. Thus the poet, speaking of the little child he met in the graveyard, writes:

> Her eyes were fair and very fair:
> Her beauty *made me glad.*
>
> W. WORDSWORTH: *We are Seven.*

But, so far, we have been speaking of the very lowest form of beauty. Beginning, then, with that which constitutes the very lowest rung of the ladder, let us strive to mount, step by step, to the highest, which is the eternal and uncreated beauty of the infinite God. Now, Lessius leads us upwards and onwards in the following manner. He invites us to begin by contemplating the most perfect and exquisite human form that has ever attracted and captivated the eyes of men. However great it may be, it is fashioned out of corruptible flesh, out of mere rude matter, and stands, therefore, at the very bottom of the series. From the beauty of visible form and colour and expression, we ascend to the more ethereal beauty of force and energy. For however splendid may be the visible beauty of gems and precious stones, of butterflies and moths and of other gaudy insects, and of animals, flowers, and of plants, in their infinite variety, their *spiritual* beauty, *which is not seen*, must be incomparably more splendid still. Let us explain. In all living and growing things, whether plants or animals, there is to be found a certain invisible but very real principle of life. For example: As I stand before a magnificent oak-tree, I may, indeed, admire and wonder at its fine proportions, at its tastefully arranged branches, and at its elaborately formed leaves, and curiously shaped fruit, and the rest. But so soon as ever I ask myself how it came to be, I must at once recognize the existence of something very much more wonderful than anything I can actually see. My reason itself goes beyond my five senses, and unhesitatingly assures me of the existence of some invisible and interior and active force, which has formed and fashioned and industriously built up the entire complicated structure now standing before me. The finest and most majestic oak in all the forest was once nothing more than an acorn—that is to say, a tiny seed. But a seed endowed by God with what seem to us almost miraculous powers. If we contemplate even a mere painted oak, we not only realize the necessity of an artist to account for its presence on the canvas, but we also realize at the same time that the artist is greater than his work—in short, that the painter is superior to his painting.

In a somewhat similar way, when contemplating, not a painted but a real oak, rearing its magnificent form in the midst of the forest, we know that it did not suddenly appear there, already fully developed, and just as we see it, but that it was gradually and slowly constructed. That which we now admire is, in short, the product of certain hidden and secret forces contained in the acorn. These forces are very real. They have exerted themselves most strenuously, year after year, with wonderful energy and perseverance. They have not only selected from earth, air, and water the appropriate and suitable materials, but they have cleverly built them up, little by little, first the blade, and then the stem, and then the branches, and then the leaves, into the perfect tree. Nothing has been done at random. Nothing is the result of mere chance. Every single branch and twig and fragment of bark and tiny rootlet has been carefully formed, according to a set plan. Every single leaf has been, so to speak, designed and carved out and shaped into the beautiful and elaborate pattern with which we are all so familiar. In this life we cannot see these wonderful forces at work. We cannot stand by and watch them going about their wonderful task, as we may watch the cotton spinners and weavers in our great manufacturing towns. But they are *just as real!* That is the point, they are quite as real, and quite as distinct from the work they do. And a day will come when God will enable us to see and admire their exceeding intrinsic beauty. Every living plant, shrub, flower, and growing thing is indebted to certain hidden, vital forces for its size, shape, colour, scent, and general character. And, if the work of these innumerable hidden forces is beautiful, and most pleasing to the eye that contemplates it, far more beautiful still, and far more interesting, will be the contemplation of these forces themselves. The living principle in a tree or a plant surpasses, no doubt, our present powers of appreciation, and we can only marvel, as we ponder over the task laid upon a seed, to construct, in its mysterious laboratory underground—let us say, a gorgeous moss-rose, or a sweet-scented pimpernel. But *the work done proves the presence of the workers* without a doubt. The effect postulates the cause. We know, with absolute certainty, that hundreds of thousands of millions of these forces exist, and that the world is full of them. Now it is the contention of theologians that the contemplation of the wondrous beauty and loveliness and attractiveness of these vital forces will be immeasurably more entrancing and joy-giving than the contemplation of anything they can produce. So that if physical and material beauty is sought after and highly appreciated, the beauty of these forces will be still more admired and will be sought after with yet greater ardour, when placed within our reach.

It stands to reason that the higher the order of the thing produced, the more wonderful and the more admirable must be the hidden forces that produce it. So that, if the vital forces in a tree or shrub possess immense beauty, the vital forces in a being of a much superior order, such as a bird or a beast, must possess a very much higher beauty still. Hence, if mere physical and material beauty forms the first or lowest rung of the ladder, and if the vital forces producing the whole vegetable world constitute the second rung, then the vital principles which are responsible for every living, breathing, and sensitive thing in the animal kingdom will form the third rung of the ladder.

Plants and trees and flowers, etc., are endowed with mere vegetable life. But, so soon as we pass on to living animals, we pass on to an immeasurably higher form of creation. The living principle in a sentient being is incomparably more wonderful and more admirable and beautiful than anything to be found in a mere plant. It is a principle not only of organic growth, but a principle of sense and of feeling and memory and motion. This living principle in every animal not only constructs such marvellous organs as eyes, ears, brain, heart, and stomach, and so forth, which are far more wonderful than anything that is to be found in a mere vegetable; but it also knows how to employ them with the utmost skill and perfection. It actually sees through the eyes, and hears through the ears, digests with the stomach, and so on with regard to every other organ in its complicated system.

From this it is clearly understood that the vital principles in the animal are of a much higher order, and of a much superior beauty, than the vital principle in the vegetable. In fact, if the beauty of all existing vegetable forms* were to be united in one individual, it would not approach the beauty of the least of the animal forms;† for the animal form is of a much higher order of creation.

A tree, or a flower, or a fruit, is a wonderful product of the forces hidden away in the seed, but if we pass from the vegetable to the animal kingdom we shall contemplate what is far more wonderful still. For a living insect, such as the bee, that gathers honey and constructs cells in which to deposit it, or a bird which enchants us with its song, or a dog which will guard our sheep-folds, is a very much more admirable and wonderful product of the forces hidden away in the egg that produces them. Let us pause here for a moment to consider the egg of any bird whatsoever. When first laid, the thin shell

* Let the unsophisticated reader understand that the term '*form*' is here and elsewhere used in the philosophical sense, and has nothing to do with '*shape*.'

† 'Anima sentiens ita est elevata supra vegetantem ut plus sit pulchritudinis in una sentiente, quam in omnibus vegetantibus simul junctis.'—L. Lessius, 'De Nom.,' p. 265.

is full of a mucous liquid, so limpid and pellucid, and apparently structureless, that, by holding it up to the sun, we can see the light pass through it. Now consider the problem to be solved by the vital forces with which the egg is endowed. Their task is to convert the liquid contained by the shell into a living, active, sensitive bird. Without adding one particle of matter from outside, these forces have to fashion every bone in the complete skeleton, give every one its required shape, and to connect them all together according to a fixed plan, with their proper joints and articulations. From the same limited liquid mass they have to form the hard beak and claws, as well as the soft down and the delicate and beautifully worked feathers that are to cover the newly born bird. Nor is that all. They have to construct, out of what is left of the same liquid, a heart that will beat, and eyes that will see, a throat and gullet and tongue and vocal chords that will really serve their purpose, as well as arteries and veins to carry blood all over the body, and to provide limbs and muscles, an alimentary canal, and a vast number of other essential parts too numerous to specify.

To form and fashion such a complicated and such a variegated object as a bird, under any conditions, might well seem an impossible task. But when the skull and bones, and beak and claws, and limbs and muscles, and heart and liver, and eyes and ears, and hundreds of beautifully woven feathers, most delicately coloured and finished, have to be manufactured from an ounce or two of mucous liquid, and arranged and built up into a highly sensitive and living creature, it seems far more impossible still. And we naturally long to see the agent that can do it. Yet this is one of the commonest operations of nature—an operation which may be witnessed a thousand times over every spring, in every part of the country.

Moreover, this marvellous transformation is brought about tranquilly and in silence, so that though you may press your ear against the shell, no sound of tool or implement can be perceived. The work is carried on with such gentleness and delicacy that even the fragile shell is not broken nor even injured in the process. Only at the appropriate moment, when the whole work is complete, is the shell forced open by the captive bird, intent on the enjoyment of its glorious liberty.

We know what was in the shell at the moment in which the egg was laid; and we know what emerges from it so soon as the egg is hatched; and we note the stupendous difference, and we rightly ascribe it to the action of the vital forces with which the Author of creation has endowed the hidden germ. We cannot actually see any of these forces, but the wonders which they perform and the visible and tangible objects which they produce declare most emphatically that they are most real. When the present life is over, and we are enabled to gaze upon these wonderful creations of Almighty God, we shall find in them a beauty and an excellence and a grace and comeliness that will far exceed the beauty and the comeliness of their visible works, which now so arrest our attention. Merely to contemplate the work achieved, as we do when we contemplate the fruits and flowers, and the birds and beasts, etc., is a joy and a delight; but, as the artist is more interesting than his work, and the painter than his picture, so the contemplation of the vital forces of nature, in all their infinite variety, will be far more wonderful and delightful than the contemplation of their visible effects.

The wonders that we have sought to illustrate by calling attention to such a simple and familiar object as a bird's egg must, of course, be applied to every living thing, from the gnat to the eagle, and from the microscopic infusoria, whose universe is a raindrop, to the antediluvian megatheria, and other gigantic extinct mammals, that once roamed about the freshly created earth.

This brings us to the fourth rung of the mystical ladder. Rising above irrational animals, we come to the rational principle in man—that is to say, the soul—made to the image and likeness of God. By means of the vital principle residing within, the *beast* is able to feel, to digest, to see and hear and smell, to run, or fly, or swim, and so forth; but by means of his rational soul, *man* can do very much more. He can think and reason, and argue and discuss; he can wonder and admire, and love and hate, and imagine and remember, and, in short, live a rational life, and exercise all the arts and crafts and sciences. Hence, even merely from its effects, we are at once brought to realize that the soul must be a truly admirable creation, and immeasurably superior to the living principle in a bird or a beast. If there are unsuspected and hidden beauties in the vegetable forces of plants, and still grander beauties in the living principles of irrational animals, there are immeasurably more enchanting beauties in the rational and immortal soul of man. In fact, if we could contemplate a single human soul, as we shall be able to contemplate it in the next life, we should find incomparably greater beauties in it than we should find in the whole of the vegetable and animal kingdoms united.* The soul of man, therefore, forms the fourth rung in the beauty-ladder. Above the soul of man stands the angelic nature of the

* 'In quarto gradu est pulchritudo animae rationalis, quae tanta est, ut quasi infinite superet omnem pulchritudinem animae sentientis. Est enim lux quaedam pura, incorporea, per se subsistens, totius universi capax.'—Lessius, 'De Summo Bono,' chap. xvi., p. 277.

heavenly hierarchy. A single human soul is something so exquisitely lovely that it eclipses all that is below it, as the sun eclipses the stars. But great as it is and splendid as it is, the pure spirit of an angel is still more captivating and attractive in its own exalted nature.

Perhaps it may be well here to recapitulate a little. Let us, then, observe that there seems to be no doubt in the minds of theologians and philosophers but that the physical beauty of fruits and flowers, however great it may be, is far surpassed by the beauty of those hidden forces which bring these very things into being. But it is important to remember that, if the forces that produce all that we admire in the vegetable world around us are so beautiful, the vital forces which produce all that we find in the still higher world of sensitive and animated nature are proportionally more beautiful still. When, however, we ascend beyond the world of living but irrational creatures, such as insects, fish, birds, and beasts, etc., to the vastly more wonderful world of rational beings, such as man, we are brought face to face with vital forces of immeasurably greater power and excellence. The human soul, which constitutes the form of the body, and which possesses not only vegetative and animal powers, but rational and intellectual powers as well, exhibits a beauty so far surpassing all other created and earthly beauties that a single soul would reveal (could we but see it) more of the splendour and the loveliness of its Maker than is to be found in all lower creatures united. This is true of a soul *before it is raised to a state of grace and glory.* When, however, a soul is lifted above nature, and raised to a supernatural state, it receives an access of beauty that eclipses every other, and which must be seen to be realized. The beauty of the angelic hosts, considered in their own nature, far outrivals the beauty of the human soul, if also considered in its own nature;* but both man and angel, when raised to a state of grace, enjoy a degree of

* 'Tota humanae naturae perfectio ad angelicam comparata, est instar nihili, et veluti punctum ad coelorum immensitatem. . . . Tamen, angelica perfectio, etiamsi absque fine in suo ordine crescat, NUNQUAM statum filiorum et gloriam ipsis praeparatam aequabit.' —'De Perf. Div.,' Lessius, p. 254.

celestial beauty that must throw *all purely natural beauty, of whatever kind,* completely into the shade. Though the purely natural beauty of either a rational soul or of an angel is inconceivably great, and beyond the power of man to imagine, yet it is paltry and contemptible as compared to the beauty of either when clothed with supernatural grace, and still more, when raised to a state of glory, for then both the one and the other actually share in the uncreated and infinite beauty of God Himself. (' Divinae consortes naturae ' —2 Pet. i. 4.)

Once the soul of man or the pure spirit of an angel has been raised to a state of glory, its beauty becomes, in a sense, divine. It is lifted up so immeasurably above all created beauty that it may truly be said to be wholly unapproachable. The great saints and writers of Mystical Theology speak of such as ' deified ' and even as ' gods,' as holy David does himself, in the Psalms, and St. Augustine, who, speaking of Heaven, says, ' Quotquot ibi sunt, dii sunt.' So that it may be truly asserted, that if every natural beauty throughout the entire universe were united in one individual, it would be just nothing at all, when compared to the beauty of the very least soul clothed in celestial glory.*

Here, then, we stand almost at the summit of the mystical ladder. There is but one beauty that can compare with the beauty of the Blessed; but one beauty that can rival and really surpass it; but one beauty that can throw it altogether in the shade—and that is the infinite and uncreated and unique and incommunicable beauty of God.

If even created beauty, in all its different stages, possesses such power to attract and to enchant, what shall we say, what can we say, of the infinite beauty of God? To be drawn within the circle of its influence is to be, at once, utterly vanquished. To catch the merest glimpse of it is to feel oneself drawn by a mighty and altogether irresistible force towards it. It is to find one's heart all aflame, and liquefying with an all-engrossing

* '(*a*) Quintus gradus est in natura angelica, quae adhuc longe sublimior ac splendidior est anima rationali; (*b*) sextus gradus est Beatorum, quorum pulchritudo superat pulchritudinem totius universi, etiamsi tota in unam formam colligatur' ('De Nom. Dei,' p. 265).

love and wonder and inexpressible delight. To gaze upon the unveiled face of God is to be filled and flooded and wholly inebriated with entrancing joy and gladness. It is to feel every fibre thrilling with exquisite joy, and every nerve vibrating and pulsating with delight, throughout our whole being. It is to plunge and to lose ourselves in a boundless sea of undreamed pleasures; to be engulfed in a bottomless ocean of ecstatic happiness—in short, it is, in very truth, to 'enter into the joy of the Lord.'

If it were possible for us fully to comprehend and to realize the entire force and meaning of the term used, it would suffice to say simply that God is '*infinitely*' more beautiful than all the works of His hands united. But since we can form no clear or adequate idea at all of the measureless contents of the term 'infinite,' we shall find it helpful to approach the contemplation of God's infinite beauty by a series of gradations, beginning with the lowest. We have already pointed them out; but, for clearness' sake, we will now set them down succinctly, and in their proper order, so that they may be taken in at a glance. To this ladder, leading up to God, there are seven rungs or steps, viz.:

I. The beauty of material and visible things, such as flowers, gems, the stars and heavenly bodies, insects, birds, animals, and men.

II. The beauty of the simple and invisible forces which God has established to fashion and build up every plant and herb and germinating thing throughout the whole *vegetable* world.

III. The beauty of the multitudinous and extremely varied principles of the higher or *animal* life, which (acting through the egg or embryo) form and give life and feeling and sense and motion to every species of living, breathing creature, in earth, air, or water.

IV. The beauty of the principle of life and *reason and intelligence* in man—in a word, the human soul.

V. The beauty of angelic beings, as exemplified in the nine choirs of angels, which are distributed into three hierarchies. Of all created beings, these are the most beautiful and exquisite, *in their own nature.* But the next or sixth step of the ladder is a very high one, and lifts us far and away beyond the fifth; for therein we pass from the *natural* to the *supernatural* order.

VI. The beauty of the beatified human soul, made to the likeness and image of God, and *clothed with grace and glory* as with a garment.

VII. The beauty of the angelic hosts, after being raised up to a state of celestial glory, and considered no longer in their own nature (beautiful though it be), but in the unrivalled beauty conferred upon them by God as a reward for their fidelity and constancy in His service, after so many of their number fell away, and were damned.

Of course, the difference in the degree of beauty between the sixth and the seventh rungs of the ladder is not so marked. In fact, they might almost be classed as one and the same; for, though no doubt many of the human race in Heaven will have less glory and therefore less beauty than even the least of the angels, yet it is the common opinion of theologians that some of the greatest of the saints may equal, even if they do not surpass, the very highest of the Seraphim and the Cherubim. On this general point the Church has made no infallible pronouncement, so we are free to form our own opinion, except in the case of our Blessed Lady; for the Church certainly holds and teaches that our Blessed Lady's soul has received far more grace and glory, and therefore far more beauty also, than even the most favoured and most exalted of the heavenly hosts. It would seem, therefore, that while the Blessed Virgin, as the glorious Mother of God, undoubtedly holds the very highest place in Heaven, the saints, according to the measure of their sanctity, will be found scattered amongst and intermingled with the various choirs of angels.

When we contemplate the beauty of the immaculate Mother of God, we contemplate a beauty beyond even that of the Cherubim and the Seraphim; for we then reach the very highest that is to be found in creatures. Yet, wonderful to say, infinitely above that dazzling and stupendous beauty rises the uncreated beauty of God—a beauty so unique, so unparalleled, and so enthralling and unfathomable, that (by comparison) no other beauty seems to deserve the name of beauty at all; in short, when placed beside the beauty of God, all other beauty is rather deformity than beauty. Oh, how inconceivable and how incomprehensible and matchless is the splendour and the glory of God!

To any adequate realization of this height we can, of course, never hope to reach in this life. But if we wish to draw just a little nearer to it, we are advised to approach it by degrees, and step by step. We should place before us the mystical ladder to which reference has already been made, and linger awhile on each rung, calling to mind the beauties that it contains. Then, before mounting to a higher rung, we should remember that each rung, except the seventh, surpasses, by an immeasurable distance, the one immediately below it. Then, by the time we have reached the topmost rung, we shall feel that beyond it there is nothing else but God Himself.

But—having exercised our minds in this way—we should then reflect that, instead of these seven rungs, God might, quite as easily, have created seven thousand or seven million rungs, each related to the other, in the same way. Yet, even then, though we should succeed in ascending to the topmost rung, we should find ourselves just as far from realizing the beauty of God as ever. For He would be as infinitely above the seven-millionth rung as above the seventh, for the simple reason that the distance between the Infinite and the finite can never be approached by any process of multiplication.

Yet—stupendous thought!—it is for the enjoyment of this uncreated, eternal, and infinite beauty of God that we are created. Well may the saints assure us that to possess and to enjoy God, even were it but for one short minute, would be a much higher privilege and an immeasurably greater honour, favour, and delight, than to swim in an ocean of earthly pleasures for a thousand years. Oh, how exceedingly should we rejoice on being invited to the nuptials of the Lamb! Even though but a very remote and uncertain chance had been afforded us, any chance at all would have been a most tremendous favour. Even though the chance given to us had been but as one to a million, yet to have received even the millionth of a chance of winning *such a prize*, would most certainly (could we but fully realize it) throw us into an ecstasy of delight, gratitude, and longing.* But, so far from making the prize difficult of attainment, or wellnigh impossible, our loving Lord has actually placed this infinite treasure so completely within the reach of every man, woman, and child, that we may truly say that if there be any one who does not attain to it, it will be wholly and entirely his own fault.

What an end to look forward to! What a consummation devoutly to be wished! Could we but realize the consoling truth, as the saints did, how impatient should we be to reach the end of the present life, and to

* Though we do not feel able to go quite the length to which Pallavicino seems to go, yet we think it will be interesting to quote his words, as given by Fra E. da Chitignano, p. 274: 'Il Pallavicino e altri sapienti in divinità, credono che sia maggiore la felicità d'un solo beato che tutte le miserie e i patimenti dell'inferno; in guisa tale, che se di tutti gli uomini da crearsi uno solo dovesse andare in paradiso e tutti gli altri all'inferno, ognuno dovrebbe desiderare di nascere in questa terra con si poca probabilità di avere ad esser egli quel solo beato, e con tanta maggior probabilità di aversi a trovare nell'immenso numero dei perduti.'—'L'Uomo in Paradiso.'

receive the imperishable crown of eternal glory. Every time we hear the clock strike the hour, we should be wont to exclaim, like St. Teresa, 'Thank God, another hour has gone by! I am brought yet another hour nearer the moment for which I long, the moment which will unite me for ever with my God and my all.' But, alas! we are not all like the saints as yet. Let us try to resemble them more nearly.

# CHAPTER V

## PARTICIPATORS IN THE DIVINE NATURE

A few more years shall roll,
  A few more seasons come,
And we shall be with those who rest
  Asleep within the tomb.

A few more struggles here,
  A few more partings o'er,
A few more toils, a few more tears,
  And we shall weep no more.

ALTHOUGH both Angels and Saints have often visited this earth, and appeared to men, yet we know but very little indeed of their celestial beauty. Even those few favoured souls who have been granted such interviews, and who have actually held converse with their heavenly visitors, have never seen, and could never have seen them *as they really are.* For no living person could possibly gaze upon a glorified soul with his corporal eyes.

When the Archangel Gabriel appeared to Daniel, he did not and could not appear as an Angel, but took the form of 'a man clothed in linen, whose loins were girded with the finest gold' (Dan. x. 5). So, too, the Archangel Raphael, who accompanied the young Tobias on his journey, was seen as 'a beautiful *young man*, girded, and as it were ready to walk,' so that 'Tobias did not at first suspect that he was an angel sent by God' (Tobias v. 5, 6). In fact, no Angel has ever shown himself to man as he is seen by his companions in Heaven. The same statement must, of course, be made likewise of the Saints in Heaven, who have from time to time visited this world. As the Saints are pure spirits, and *as yet without any body*, they can no more appear in their true glorified state than can the Angels themselves, but must assume, for the time being, some form that mortal man can bear to gaze upon, for no human being in his mortal state could bear the brightness and the beauty of a soul, in all its unveiled glory, and live. St. Bridget declares that if we were to see an Angel as he really is, we should die of sheer delight; and that if we were to see a devil as he really is, we should die of horror and terror.*

It has often been asserted by mystical writers, that if God were to strengthen us, so that we could, without dying of wonder and admiration, behold even the very least of His glorified Saints in all his celestial beauty and glory, our first impression would be that we were contemplating God Himself. And this seems probable enough. If a glorified soul were to appear to us, we should find ourselves gazing upon a beauty surpassing, by an immeasurable degree, every beauty hitherto known to us, and of a superior order. It would be a beauty so transcendent that we should not be able even to conceive a greater. Hence we should naturally exclaim within ourselves, 'Surely this must be the limit! I cannot believe anything more lovely or more exquisite can exist! Surely there can be nothing to surpass this! I must be gazing at God Himself.' In a word, before growing conscious of our mistake, we should require to be assured, on Divine authority, that this beauty, so fascinating and so en-

* See Poulain, 'Graces d'Oraison,' p. 314.

trancing us, is infinitely less than the uncreated beauty of God—that, in sober truth, it is, after all, nothing more than the beauty of one of the least of His favoured servants.

Something akin to this actually happened to St. John, even though he had already had so many and such wonderful visions. For he tells us, in the Apocalypse, that when the glorious angel stood before him, to reveal the secrets of God—'I fell down before his feet *to adore him*. But he said to me: See thou do it not; I am thy fellow-servant, and of thy brethren, who have the testimony of Jesus. Adore God.' St. Augustine remarks that 'the angel was so beautiful and glorious that St. John *actually mistook him for God*, and would really have given him Divine worship, had not the angel prevented it, by declaring who he was.' Yet there can be no doubt but that St. John did not see the angel in his full and naked beauty, as the blessed see him now in Heaven (see Apoc. xix. 10). What he saw was, after all, but an 'appearance.'

If, then, such be the marvellous splendour and entrancing loveliness of even the very least in the Kingdom of Heaven, what must be the beauty of the greatest and the most exalted? And what shall we say of the incalculable sum of beauty of all Saints and all Angels taken together, especially considering their inconceivable number, which defies all calculation. 'Count, if you can,' says the great Bossuet, 'the sands on the sea-shore, count if you can the stars in the firmament, and when you have done so, be firmly convinced that you have not reached the number of the Angels.' Speaking only of one section —namely, of those whose duty it is to assist before the throne of God—Daniel, in inspired words, tells us that, 'Thousands upon thousands minister to Him, and ten hundred times a hundred thousand assist before His Throne.'

Yet in spite of this, there can be no doubt but that it is not so much their prodigious number as their extraordinary variety that will fill us with delight. Cardinal Newman compares the variety of beauty among the Saints of God's Church to the variety of beauty observable among the flowers in a sumptuous garden. Though his words refer to the Saints alone, yet they are perhaps even still more applicable to the Angels, if we accept St. Thomas's teaching, and may certainly be made to embrace both the one and the other. 'Each,' he says, 'has his own distinguishing grace, apart from the rest, and his own particular hue and fragrance and fashion, as a flower may have. As there are numerous flowers on the earth, all of them flowers, and so far, like each other; and all springing from the same earth, and nourished by the same air and dew, and none without beauty; and yet some are more beautiful than others; and of those which are beautiful, some excel in colour, and others in sweetness and others in form; and then again, those which are sweet have such perfect sweetness, yet so distinct, that we do not know how to compare them together, or to say which is the sweeter; so is it with souls filled and nurtured by God's secret grace.'* And so, let me add, is it likewise, only in a yet higher degree, with the countless angelic spirits which fill the heavenly courts with their dazzling beauty.

But how, it may be asked, shall we ever be

* Newman's 'Parochial and Plain Sermons,' p. 55.

able to so much as make the acquaintance of such vast hosts of Angels and of Saints? It would be impossible, of course, were we to be left in our present helplessness, but God will so strengthen our minds and so enlarge our faculties that we shall know each and every one with the utmost perfection. Even in this present life God has sometimes conferred this extraordinary knowledge upon some of His Saints, to their great delight. Thus, for instance, we are assured by St. Alphonsus Rodriguez that being, on one occasion, transported, like another St. Paul, to Heaven, he not only saw all the inhabitants of that celestial region, but saw each one quite distinctly, and knew each individual as perfectly as if he had passed the whole of his life in his company.* Much the same favour was often conferred on St. Bridget.

* 'Dans les visions il peut y avoir beaucoup de connaissances simultanées. St. Alphonse Rodriguez raconte qu'étant transporté au ciel, il vit et connut TOUS les bienheureux ensemble, et chacun d'eux distinctement, comme s'il eût passé TOUTE SA VIE AVEC EUX. . . . On raconte que St. Brigitte voyait souvent, en un seul instant, tous les habitants du ciel, de la terre et de l'enfer, *et ce qu'ils se disaient les uns aux autres.*' (See Poulain's 'Graces d'Oraison,' p. 326.)

If Saints on earth can receive such powers, and do such things, we may be quite sure that souls in Heaven will not be less favoured, but will be enriched with even greater powers, and do yet more wonderful things. Although the ravishing beauty and splendour of the innumerable Saints and Angels, our beloved companions and most devoted and intimate friends and associates, will add enormously to the happiness of our existence in that thrice blessed Land, yet even such overpowering happiness is quite secondary, and forms no part of the *essential* happiness of Heaven. The company of such choice spirits is to be reckoned only as one among what are called the 'accidental' joys; I say 'one,' because these accidental joys are many. Yet although they are both innumerable and ineffable, they cannot for a moment bear any comparison to the joy arising from the clear contemplation and the complete possession of God Himself. And this is a point of such transcendently practical importance, that it will be well to offer a few remarks concerning it.

Though all well-instructed Catholics realize

that God must, from the very nature of the case, be the one supreme and only infinite source of happiness, yet not one in a hundred at all understands the close and personal union that takes place in Heaven between the vast Creator and His poor insignificant little creatures—*i.e.*, between God and the soul—though this constitutes the very essence and marrow of the whole situation.

They know that God is essentially One and Indivisible, and infinitely greater than even the sublimest of His creatures. But as a direct consequence of this knowledge, they persuade themselves that no individual can ever approach very near to Him. They fancy that they, and all the rest of the Blessed, will contemplate Him merely from afar, and that although their celestial happiness, of course, consists in gazing upon His beauty and perfections, it will be in gazing at them *from a respectful distance.* They seem to picture themselves to themselves as seated upon heavenly thrones (as they might be seated in the stalls of a theatre), to look upon some entrancing scene; or as men on earth might gaze upon some newly discovered star. To be allowed even such a distant and partial view of God's infinite beauty, were it all we had to look forward to, might be a signal favour, but it is nothing to the glorious reality.

What 'the man in the street' forgets is that, although God is truly one and indivisible, yet that this self-same One and Indivisible God may be, and indeed is, equally present, wholly and entirely, in every point of space, and what is more, that He gives Himself wholly and entirely to each individual soul in Heaven, just as though that individual were the only soul in existence. Each of the Blessed possess Him as completely as if He were present to no other. God actually unites Himself, in an ineffable manner, to each of the saved. Wonderful to say, each actually shares in the life of God; feels, as it were, His breath; thrills beneath His touch; and pours forth praises, adorations, and thanksgivings into His ear, as some perfect instrument distils sweet music in the hands of a skilled musician. No words can, in truth, describe the intimacy and the closeness of the union between God and His sweet spouse, the purified and glorified soul, or even suggest the raptures and the transports of His eternal embrace.

Even though this statement may strike us as marvellous and as almost too good to be true, yet the doctrine of the Holy Eucharist ought to be enough to prepare our minds to accept it, and to pave the way for a hearty and most grateful act of faith.

In Holy Communion each one of the many millions of communicants receives into his soul, not only the entire Body and Blood and human soul of Jesus Christ, but His Divinity also; and (by *circumincessio*) the three Divine Persons of the adorable Trinity, the Father, Son, and Holy Ghost, likewise. For, by reason of Their identity with the one indivisible Substance and of Their essential relations to each other, none of Them can be conceived without or separate from the other Two.* So that, whether I am alone, or whether I am but one of many thousands, I receive absolutely the same. As St. Thomas sings: 'Sumunt unus, sumunt mille; quantum isti, tantum ille'; the number makes no

* See Wilhelm and Scannell, 'Manual of Theology,' vol. i., p. 264.

difference. If, then, such are our privileges *here, during our exile on earth,* what will they not be in our Father's Home in Heaven? Although hidden from our view, yet even *in this world,* God condescends to come to us, in all His glory and majesty, and to dwell in the centre of our soul, whenever we approach the altar rails. So intimate is that bond that we may then truthfully exclaim: 'I live, now not I, but Christ liveth in me' (Gal. ii. 20). This being the case, we may surely well ask: will God treat us with less familiarity and condescension when our period of trial and probation is over and our salvation is secured? Assuredly not! That which He does for us now, while we are *in via,* is but an earnest of immeasurably greater favours, to be heaped upon us when we are *in Patria*—*i.e.,* safe in our Father's Home. In Heaven He will give Himself to each one of us, we cannot say in a *truer* way than upon earth, but in a far more sensible and manifest way, so that we shall be able fully to appreciate and to relish all the undreamed-of sweetness and fragrance of His presence. In Holy Communion our eyes are holden, our senses shut up, and our mind is left in darkness, illuminated solely by the obscure glimmer of faith. In Heaven our eyes shall be wide open, and our soul will actually gaze upon and realize the infinite beauty and divine perfections of Him who holds us in His eternal and all-embracing love. No exercise of faith will be any longer needed, for then faith will have been changed into the clearest vision, so that the presence of God in the soul will be felt and enjoyed and understood, as it never can be on earth. For as the Saints have expressed it, 'we shall be immersed and penetrated and filled by the Divine immensity, as a sponge in the ocean is saturated and filled by its brimming waters.'

God will act in us, and through us, and with us. He will impart to us a share in His own Divine attributes, and will flood our whole being with His own perfections, very much as the fierce fire, in a blazing furnace, will fill and flood with its own bright light and heat the iron bar that is cast into its transforming flames. Such, at all events, is one of the commonest illustrations with which spiritual writers have sought to interpret St. Peter's bold words, that we are to be made 'partakers of the divine nature' (2 Pet. i. 4).

Speaking of the happiness of the Saints in glory, Bishop G. Bautista de Lanuza, O.P., writes: 'God will give Himself wholly to the soul, with all His substance, omnipotence, glory, majesty, eternity, wisdom, wealth, etc., in such a way that nothing will belong to God that does not belong to the soul. (These will form the real riches of the soul) for the soul will possess these divine gifts in a far truer and more intimate way than the rich and noble of this world may be said to 'possess' the gold and silver and all the earthly treasures that they boast of, and claim as their own. In short, just as the soul, united to the body, communicates to it life and vigour and motion, so, but in a much more ineffable manner, God united to the soul will communicate to it His divine attributes and infinite perfections. 'Ut impleamini in omnem plenitudinem Dei.'

As these startling words may astonish some of my readers, who may think that I am exaggerating, I append the Bishop's sentences just as they are, in the original

Spanish.* What Lessius teaches is very similar, though expressed in different and even stronger words.†

Before ascending to His heavenly Father, our Divine Lord made known to His disciples that He was going to prepare for them a

* 'Todo Dios se dará al alma con toda su sustancia, omnipotencia, gloria, magestad, eternidad, sabiduría, riqueza; de manera, que nada tendrá Dios que no sea del alma; y tan suyo, que lo poseerá en sí misma, y lo encerrará dentro de si; mas suyo sin comparacion que el oro y la plata, las heredades y posesiones de la tierra, y aun los propios vestidos que no pueden entra en el corazon, ni encerrarse en él. A la manera que el alma está dentro del cuerpo comunicándole el sér, la vida y el movimiento, así de un modo mas inefable estará Dios en el alma comunicándola su divino sér y sus perfecciones infinitas; Ut impleamini in omnem plenitudinem Dei' (Ephes. iii. 19).—Lanuza, 'Discursos Praedicables,' A.D. 1803, tom. vi. 73.

† 'Ad divinam pulchritudinem et speciem, quae prorsus inaestimabilis et infinita est, proxime accedit pulchritudo animae beatae, quae *Deo adeo est similis, ut nulla major cum Deo similitudo vel animo concipi, vel etiam per potentiam Dei absolutam* (ut valde probabile est) dari possit; ut merito dictum sit a Sto. Joanne; cum apparuerit, similis ei erimus, quoniam videbimus eum sicuti est. Ratio est, quia in statu beatitudinis erit suprema participatio divinarum perfectionum; imo ipsa beatitudo in tali communicatione consistit.'—L. Lessius, 'De Summo Bono,' l. ii., chap. xvi., p. 278.

celestial banquet in Heaven, where they would not only enjoy His company, but where they would even 'sit at His table, and eat and drink with Him.' Under this familiar figure He taught them that they would share in His own delights, derive happiness from the same source, and be nourished by the same spiritual food, or, as St. Thomas expresses it, 'Super mensam Dei manducant et bibunt, quia eadem felicitate fruuntur qua Deus felix est, videntes eum illo modo quo ipse videt seipsum.'* Our thoughts recur to this promise when we contemplate the Angel 'standing in the sun,' spoken of by St. John in the Apocalypse, 'who cried with a loud voice, Come and gather yourselves together to the great supper of God' (xix. 17). At that heavenly banquet we shall feast on, and be, as it were, filled and inebriated with, the divinity. For there we shall see God, and be with God, and shall live by God. As St. Bernard writes: 'Praemium nostrum est videre Deum, esse cum Deo, vivere de Deo.' There, in a word, will be consummated, and made perfect and perpetual, the holy union,

* 'Contra Gent.,' I. iii., cap. li.

now only begun, between the soul and God, a union so close and so ineffable as to fill the soul with ecstasy for all eternity. There, the heavenly Bridegroom will invite His chosen spouse to eat and drink of the celestial food, and to share in all the supernatural festivities and pleasures suggested by a superb and unexampled celestial marriage feast.

The beatitude of the next life may be likened to some priceless elixir, but with this difference, that the elixir is stored in tiny vases, and is so soon exhausted that it has to be carefully dealt out in carefully measured drops, whereas the beatitude of Heaven is poured forth without measure or limit, and flows, not like a quiet, steady stream, but as a veritable 'torrent'; as it were rushing and tumultuous and overflowing its banks through the very abundance and copiousness of its volume. Men will not only 'drink,' but they will be, as the inspired writer expresses it, inebriated and intoxicated with the intensity of their pleasure. 'Inebriabuntur ab ubertate domus Tuae, et torrente voluptatis Tuae potabis eos' (Ps. xxxv. 9).

'As a draught diffuses itself through all the

members and veins of the body, so this communication of God diffuses itself substantially in the whole soul, or, rather, the soul is transformed in God. In this transformation the soul drinks of God in its very substance and its spiritual powers. In the intellect it drinks wisdom and knowledge, in the will the sweetest love, in the memory refreshment and delight, in the thought and sense glory unspeakable. That the soul receives and drinks delight in its very substance, appears from the words of the Bride in the Canticle: "My soul melted, when He spoke"—that is, when the Bridegroom communicated Himself to the soul.'* 'This Divine draught deifies the soul, and elevates and inebriates it in God.'†

Theologians distinguish between two sorts of 'participation in the Divine nature.' The first confers upon the soul a certain resemblance to God, so that this participation is brought about *per quamdam similitudinis participationem;* the second consists in an intimate union between the soul and God. The two sorts of participation are mentioned and

* 'St. John of the Cross,' vol. ii., p. 140.
† *Ibid.*, p. 141.

treated as united by St. Dionysius, when he writes: 'Est autem haec deificatio ad Deum, quanta fieri potest, (1) assimilatio *et* (2) unio.' No one can sound the depths of this sublime mystery or conceive the closeness of such a union.

St. Teresa compares this union between God and the soul, (1) to the water which falls from the skies into a fountain, which mingle together in such a way that *one cannot distinguish the one from the other*, and (2) to a little brook that flows into the ocean, so that the waters of each become indistinguishable, and also (3) to the light coming into a room through two different windows, which unite in such a manner as to seem to be *exactly one and the same.* The natures of God and of the soul are so united, says St. John of the Cross, and what is Divine is so communicated to what is human, that, without undergoing any essential change, *each seems to be God*' (p. 120). The soul actually reposes between the arms of its heavenly Bridegroom, whose spiritual embraces are so real that it now, through them, lives the life of God. Now is fulfilled what St. Paul referred to when he said: 'I live; now not I, but Christ liveth in me.' And now that the soul lives a life so happy and so glorious as this life of God, consider what a life it must be—a life where God sees nothing displeasing, and where the soul finds nothing irksome, but rather the glory and delight of God in the very substance of itself, now transformed in Him' (vol. ii., stanza xxii., p. 121).

Nothing in this world can be cited as a really adequate illustration. The example or illustration actually inspired by the Holy Ghost Himself, in more than one place, in the pages of Holy Scripture, is that of marriage. For marriage is the very closest union recognized by us mortals on earth; though it must be confessed that even marriage falls immeasurably short of being a really adequate figure. The spiritual, or what is more commonly called the mystical, marriage is a union between God and the soul, close, intimate, profound, and eternal, and immeasurably surpassing, in every respect, that which exists between husband and wife; for the operations of Nature can never offer us anything better than the faintest shadow of the sublime operations of Grace. In the one case the union is but a corporal one, in the other it is wholly spiritual. In the one case it involves but a material contact, in the other the whole soul is permeated and penetrated and taken possession of by God.* Hence, while the Apostle, in inspired words, describes the spouses of an earthly marriage as '*two in one flesh,* the same Apostle describes the spiritual marriage of the soul and God as TWO IN ONE SPIRIT,' saying: 'Qui adhaeret Domino, unus spiritus efficitur' (1 Cor. vi. 17).

In this connection it may be well to recall the words of St. John of the Cross, who reminds us of the prayer which Our Divine Lord addressed to His heavenly Father for His followers, asking 'that they may be one, as

* 'Union pleine de douceur et de suavité. Comparée à cette union sainte, l'union matrimoniale n'est que froideur et amertume. Ici, le contentement est court, le plaisir bas et grossier; là, tout est grand, élevé, durable; c'est la gloire, c'est la pureté, c'est la tendresse, ce sont d'ineffables délices que la langue humaine est incapable d'exprimer, et le cœur de l'homme trop étroit pour les contenir.'—'De L'Habitation du Saint-Esprit,' p. 297, R. P. Froget.

Thou, Father, in Me, and I in Thee, that they also may be one in Us. . . . And the glory which Thou hast given Me, I have given to them; that they may be one as We also are one.' He then goes on to warn us that 'we are not to suppose from this that Our Lord prayed that the Saints might become one in essence and natural unity, as the Father and the Son are; but that they might become one in the union of love, as the Father and the Son are one in the oneness of their love. Thus souls have this great blessing *by participation* which the Son has *by nature*, and are therefore *really gods by participation, like unto God, and of His nature.*'*

It seems strange, and at first sight almost incredible, that God should love so intensely a poor imperfect human creature, and that He should treat him with so much real affection. St. John of the Cross seems to explain this difficulty in some measure by reminding us that God first clothes the soul with His own beauty and so loves Himself as He contemplates His image in the soul, and becomes enamoured of all His own Divine perfections,

* Vol. ii., pp. 204-5.

which are mirrored there, as in a glass. Further, the glorified soul, on its side, being made by grace a most speaking image of God, will see its own image and its own beauty in God, and will greatly rejoice to behold in God the eternal and infinite reality, of which it itself is but the created and finite and unworthy expression or reflection. In the following words of St. John of the Cross I think we may gather this meaning, although the language, thus translated (by David Lewis), is a little involved and difficult to follow. Describing the soul, about to enter into Heaven, he represents it as addressing God in the following manner: ' " I shall see Thee in Thy beauty, and myself in Thy beauty, and Thou shalt see me in Thy beauty; and I shall see myself in Thee in Thy beauty, and Thou Thyself in me in Thy beauty; so *shall I seem to be Thyself* in Thy beauty and Thou myself in Thy beauty. My beauty shall be Thine, Thine shall be mine, and I shall be Thou in it, and Thou myself in Thine own beauty; for *Thy beauty will be my beauty,* and so we shall see, each the other, in Thy beauty." This is the adoption of the sons of God, who may truly say what the Son Himself says to the Eternal Father: "All My things are Thine, and Thine are Mine" (John xvii. 10); He by essence (being the Son of God by nature), we by participation (being sons by adoption).'*

St. John writes in the third chapter of his first Epistle: '*We know that when He shall appear we shall be like to Him, because we shall see Him as He is.*' Now, commenting upon this passage, the late Bishop Hedley, O.S.B., observes: 'The words "*when He shall appear*," signify the judgment and the entrance into Heaven; to "*see Him as He is*" expresses the Beatific Vision; and the phrase "*we shall be like to Him*" is the Apostle's announcement that before we can see God, He must have taken possession of our whole being; His glory must have transfigured our being; and we must have been so gifted that it may be as it were *God Himself who looks upon Himself*,'† which comes very much to what St. John of the Cross says.

Thus it is made clear that the transcendent joy which floods the entire soul in Heaven

* Vol. ii., p. 187.

† *Vide* Bishop Hedley's 'Retreat,' p. 402.

is no other than the joy of God Himself. 'Enter thou into the joy of thy Lord.' The joy which constitutes the bliss of God, and by which He is essentially and eternally happy, is the very same joy which He communicates to us in Heaven when He shows us His infinite beauty. 'I am thy reward exceeding great' (Gen. xv. 1); 'I am thy salvation' (Ps. xxxiv. 3). God is a Being infinitely great, infinite in all possible perfections. And the enjoyment of His infinite beauty, which is manifested in all His Divine perfections, is so exquisitely delightful as to render God Himself completely and infinitely happy for all eternity. Yet, wonderful to relate, this infinite happiness, this exquisite delight which God possesses in Himself is precisely that which He communicates to us in His heavenly kingdom, to the full extent of our finite capacity. He will not say simply, 'Enter into joy,' but, to show the exalted character of that joy, He says: 'Enter into the *joy of thy Lord*'—into that joy which God Himself possesses and which is such as to render even that Infinite Being infinitely happy. As a consequence, the joy of the

Blessed from the Beatific Vision of the Divine beauty must be wholly unutterable, and all the delights of this world, by comparison, nothing but bitterness, gall and wormwood. So incomprehensible is their joy that thousands of years pass away like a day, and each day gives them the joy of thousands of years, 'Be not ignorant, my beloved,' says St. Peter. 'that one day with the Lord is as a thousand years, and a thousand years as one day' (2 Pet. iii. 8). Holy David also assures us that 'a thousand years in the sight of God are but as yesterday, which is passed and gone' (Ps. lxxxiii. 11). Wonderful statements which help us to form some idea of the amazing delight which must flow from the contemplation of God.*

Another characteristic of heavenly joy, which distinguishes it from all earthly joys of every description, is the fact that it never wearies nor grows stale. Although every power and faculty of the soul shall be perfectly filled and satisfied with it, and although man's whole being shall be satiated with the most indescribable delights, and although

* *Vide* Dr. Hay's 'Devout Christian,' p. 116.

this shall continue, without a moment's interruption, for the whole of an exhaustless eternity, yet the soul will never grow in the least weary of it—never tire of it, or seek any change; will never loathe it, or be cloyed with it. Quite the contrary, she will discover in the Divine beauty an inexhaustible fountain of perfections, of wonders, of truths, of graces, and will be so totally overwhelmed with the ineffable joy she experiences in beholding it that for all eternity she will never be able to turn her thoughts, no, not for a single moment, from contemplating the entrancingly lovely object which causes it. And, what is more, her delight will continue to be as full, as entire, as intense, and as inconceivably great throughout all eternity, as it was the first moment she entered into possession of it.

What a contrast this offers us to the wretched pleasures of this world, the very highest and best of which cannot be enjoyed but for a short time without engendering the most unmistakable disgust and loathing.

The contemplation of Heaven, and of the wonders which God has prepared for those who love Him, is calculated to impress the mind of the believer very deeply. Perhaps the first impression will be one of wonder and admiration at the inconceivable grandeur and wholly unimaginable range and magnificence of that life of union with God. The second will be one of gratitude and thankfulness to God, whose condescension, generosity, and love is thereby so abundantly manifested. It will come to us as a fresh proof of the marvellous tenderness, compassion, and infinite goodness of our heavenly Father, and our hearts will burn with love for One who is prepared to treat us with such infinite honour and distinction, affection and familiarity.

But the most deeply marked impression, I take it, will be one of almost incredible astonishment that such and so unique a future should actually be within our reach. It almost makes one stagger, and takes one's breath away, to think, and not only to think, but to *know with all the certainty of faith*, that such a future is actually offered to us, and on the easiest conditions, and that we shall really and truly secure it, if only we lead ordinary good lives. The contrast between that celestial life and the present life is so immense, its occupations, its surroundings, its society and environment, so totally unlike anything to which we have been accustomed, that we can hardly bring ourselves to realize that we can ever be so far exalted above our present lowly state as to become courtiers of the King of kings and Lord of lords, yea, the loved and spoiled children of the infinite Being Who created us, and Whose love is the richest and the highest of all possessions. 'To Whom be benediction, and glory, and wisdom, and thanksgiving, honour, power, and strength, for ever and ever' (Apoc. vii. 12).

## CHAPTER VI

## THE DESIRE TO BE DISSOLVED

It must be so—*Plato*, thou reason'st well—
Else whence this pleasing hope, this fond desire,
This longing after Immortality ?
Or whence this secret dread, and inward horror,
Of falling into naught ? Why shrinks the soul
Back on herself, and startles at destruction ?
'Tis the divinity that stirs within us;
'Tis heav'n itself that points out an hereafter,
And intimates eternity to man.

Reason informs me I shall never die.
The soul, secur'd in her existence, smiles
At the drawn dagger, and defies its point.
The stars shall fade away, the sun himself
Grow dim with age, and nature sink in years;
But thou shalt flourish in immortal youth,
Unhurt amidst the war of elements,
The wrecks of matter, and the crush of worlds.

J. ADDISON.

Leve est mihi omne onus, quod fero,
propter magnum illud bonum, quod spero.

ST. FRANCIS.

TO die is quite as natural as to be born. And there is, from many points of view, a great similarity between birth and death. Both involve a sudden and a radical change. Both experiences are attended with some degree of pain; both mark the passage from a less to a more perfect condition of life, and both introduce us into a fuller and a more extended field of action. If a man could think and reason during the months of his pre-natal existence, he would probably imagine the life of which he then has experience to be the only life he will ever enjoy, and that the cataclysm of birth will mean for him annihilation. Yet, in the fullness of time, he emerges into a world far more wonderful and far more beautiful than anything he ever dreamed of; an experience, indeed, for which the previous months of his existence have been nothing more than a necessary preparation. So is it with that final birth which we call death. Though we may fear it, and imagine it to be the final end of our existence, yet it is, in truth, but the natural means by which we are ushered into yet another world, immeasurably more wonderful and beautiful than that into which our first birth admitted us. In fact, in this sense, we may surely say:

> There is no death! What seems so
> is transition;
> This life of mortal breath is but a suburb
> of the life Elysian
> Whose portal we call death.

Catholics, at all events, know that to one who has served God loyally, death is nothing more than the dark and dreaded entry into a new world of such untold glory and splendour as to beggar all description.

So soon as he grows conscious of his immortality, man realizes that the present life is nothing more than a passing incident in a career which can have no end, and he awaits the next stage with immense interest and with the brightest and most glorious expectations.

Since death is a punishment and a penalty justly inflicted by God on man, on account of sin, it is only right and proper that he should stand in some fear of it; and, so long as men are in good health, this fear is generally acknowledged. But when the moment of departure from this world actually draws near, this fear, in almost every case, disappears. Cardinal Manning's explanation of the phenomenon was a very simple one. He said to me one day, when conversing on the subject: 'The reason, I take it, is this: so long as God *intends a man to live,* He instils into him the fear of death; when He *intends him to die,* He mercifully withdraws this fear, so that most persons, at the very last, deliver up their souls into the hands of God as peacefully and as calmly as a healthy child composes himself to sleep.'

I have questioned scores of priests and doctors and nurses, and they have all assured me that their experience has been much the same, though they did not offer the explanation offered by the Cardinal. Dr. Robert W. Mackenna writes:

'Personally, I have never seen anyone about to die evince the slightest fear of the impending change, and this experience is supported by a great body of weighty medical opinion. Sir Benjamin Brodie, who a century ago was the acknowledged *doyen* of surgery in England, has left the following record in one of his conversational essays: "I have myself never known but two instances in which, in the act of dying, there were manifest indications of the fear of death." Now,

Brodie was a man of very wide experience, which ranged through every social grade, from Windsor Castle to the slums of London, and in his day he must have seen many people die. But only two—an infinitesimal proportion of the whole—showed fear.*

'I have fought with death,' writes Dr. Mackenna, 'and lost the battle, over the beds of young men and women in the first flush of maturity; I have seen strong men and women cut down in their prime; I have watched the old totter down the slope, into the twilight, and at the end fall asleep like little children, and I say it, with a due sense of the importance of the statement, that my experience has been that, however much men and women may, when in the full vigour of health, fear death, when their hour approaches the fear is almost invariably lulled into quietness, and they face the end with calmness and a serene mind.' †

Dr. Mackenna reports many instances. I will quote just one: 'A young man who fell from the roof of a lofty building and escaped

* See 'The Adventure of Death,' pp. 70, 71.

† *Ibid.*, p. 63.

miraculously, with a handful of bruises, assured me that, in his long fall to earth, which seemed to cover an eternity, he did not feel the slightest fear; and I have been told by three medical men, each of whom narrowly escaped drowning under *entirely different circumstances*, that when their fate seemed certain, all fear was taken from them.'* 'If I had strength enough to hold a pen,' said Dr. W. Hunter, just before he expired, 'I would write down how easy and pleasant a thing it is to die.' Another celebrated physician, Sir J. F. Goodhart, who made a *special study of death scenes*, gives his experiences, in the following words: 'I am never tired of saying, because I am sure it is as true as it is comforting, although in opposition to the general belief, that death has no terror for the sick man. There is nothing terrible to the dying in death itself. The veil between the two worlds is but a cloud, and one passes through it imperceptibly.'†

Mechnikov, the illustrious Russian biologist, believed that 'as science banished disease

* See 'The Adventure of Death,' p. 67.
† *Ibid.*, p. 72.

and as reasonable habits of life prevented the various forms of auto-intoxication, natural old age would be as serene and beautiful as are healthy childhood, youth, and maturity. He elaborated the theory that, just as the child longs to grow up and the boy or girl wishes to be adult, so, if it arrived only in the natural way and in the natural time, death would no longer be feared, but would be awaited with calm satisfaction.'*

As a straw shows which way the wind blows, so the following little dialogue, to be met with in Mrs. H. Wood's well-known story of 'Johnny Ludlow,' seems to show how universal the experience is. A dying son is represented as so calm and peaceful and resigned, that his weeping mother addresses him: 'And don't you *care* to leave us?' 'I *did* care very much; but lately I seem to have looked only to the time when we shall meet again. Mother, *I do not think now I would live even if the chance were offered me.* . . .' 'Well, it is the first time I ever heard of young people wanting to die.' 'Mother! I think we must be very close to death *before*

* See *The Times*, July 25, 1922, p. 12.

we want it. . . . Don't you see the mercy ? —that *when this world is passing from us, we are led insensibly to long for the next.*' (*Vide* p. 464.)

If such be the case with ordinary men, whose lives are marked by no special piety and holiness, it is far truer still of those whose vivid faith and personal worthiness have been much above the average. The Saint and the devout and loyal servant of God, who has pondered over the inspired words of Holy Scripture, and whose mind is filled with thoughts of the wonderful rewards which God has prepared for those who love Him, not only meets death with calmness and resignation, but often with a great longing and an intense joy.

He feels that, in spite of many imperfections and even daily faults, he has honestly and sincerely striven to live for God alone. He has unbounded confidence in the infinite compassion, mercy, and pity of his divine Master, and he knows that He desires his salvation more even than he does himself, and that He will grant forgiveness of his faults of surprise, of frailty, and weakness, more readily than he is ready to ask forgiveness. And lying there, on his death-bed at last, he feels the greatest confidence, for he knows Whom he has trusted, and he firmly believes that Christ, Who died for him, amid such atrocious tortures, will now stretch forth His Divine arms to welcome him as a son redeemed by His precious Blood, and receive him into eternal rest, as the choice fruit of His sacred Passion.

On one occasion, St. Teresa, while suffering great pain, expressed herself as follows: 'The pain seems to me sharp enough to cause death; *only I do not deserve it.* All my anxiety at these times is that I should die; I do not think of Purgatory, nor of the great sins I have committed, and by which I have deserved hell. I forget everything, in my eagerness to see God.'* 'Oh,' she exclaims, on another occasion, 'sometimes I consider, if a person like myself frequently feels her banishment so much, what the feelings of the Saints must have been. What must St. Paul and the Magdalene, and others like them, have suffered, in whom the fire of the

* 'Life,' p. 149.

love of God had grown so strong? *Their life must have been a continual martyrdom.*'* When at last (some years later) she lay on her death-bed, her heart began to overflow with joy at the prospect of being united with God, When the Viaticum was brought to her, she could scarcely contain herself. Her biographer records that—

'In spite of her extreme exhaustion, which for two days had prevented her making the slightest movement, she raised herself in bed to a kneeling posture, and would have knelt on the ground unless she had been prevented. Her look became inflamed, her face lit up with a heavenly brightness, and her whole being was transformed. Then, with a loud and vibrating voice, she cried, "Oh! my Lord, and my well-beloved Spouse! The longed-for hour is arrived. It is time we should see each other. Oh! my Saviour and my only love, it is time to depart; it is time I should go out of this life. Blessed a thousand times be this hour, and may Thy will be accomplished. Yes; the hour is arrived when my soul shall go to Thee, to

* 'Life,' p. 161.

be united to Thee, after waiting for Thee so long."*

'Her agony began without groans, or sighs, or sufferings; joyous, as if rapt in ecstasy, she lay in her Saviour's arms, waiting for the moment when Heaven should open to receive her. . . . The little cell had become a place of paradise. An ever increasing brightness dwelt on the saint's countenance. Her features were invested with a supernatural beauty. The rays of light which encircled her forehead, the crimson on her cheeks, the unutterable joy of her expression, were all divine. God was present there, and His beloved already enjoyed a foretaste of the joys of the blessed. Towards nine in the evening three gentle sighs escaped her, so soft that they resembled rather those made by a person absorbed in prayer than one in her agony, and she gave up her soul to God.' †

We have another illustration in the death of St. Peter of Alcantara:

'When he knew that the most holy Viaticum

* Deposition made by Sister Mary of St. Francis. V. de la Fuente.

† 'Life,' p. 603.

was coming, although weakened, and like a paralytic unable to move, he threw himself at once, without any assistance, on his knees, and with clasped hands and incredible fervour of spirit, worshipped the Blessed Sacrament, and received it with the greatest veneration, with tears and holy awe, and begged that at the proper time he might receive the most holy Sacrament of Extreme Unction. Then, fixing his eyes on the crucifix, with a serene countenance, and his spirit as it were on fire, he remained for some time in profound repose, in an ecstasy, and absorbed in God. When the physician came, the dying man asked him: "When will the longed-for time come, and the hour when I shall be delivered from this destruction, and shall enter on the way of life?" The physician replied: "Father, that hour will soon come, it is now drawing nigh." When the holy man heard this, he was affected with unutterable joy, and turning exultingly to God, he repeated with a joyous look the words of the royal prophet: "I rejoiced at the things that were said to me; we shall go into the house of the Lord." '*

* *Vide* 'Report of the Auditors of the Rota.'

When Cardinal Wiseman was on his death-bed, he is reported to have said that he had no misgivings, but that he felt full of joy, '*like a schoolboy going home.*' And we have all, no doubt, heard of the great theologian Suarez's last words. Though during life he had almost an abnormal fear of death, yet, when it was actually on him, he smiled, and his whole face lit up, as he exclaimed: '*Oh! I little thought how sweet a thing it is to die.*' A few years ago a holy religious, whose name I am not at liberty to mention, was dying, and I am assured by one who was present that one of his companions talking quietly to him, just after he had received Extreme Unction, asked him if he were not terrified at the thought of meeting our Divine Lord. Upon which he seemed to be quite astonished, and replied: 'What? Terrified to meet Our Lord? Afraid to meet Him Whom I have served and laboured for during the past forty years, and Who is charity itself? What? Afraid to meet *Him?* Certainly not; *I would be much more afraid to meet the Provincial!*'

Death may be regarded from two very different points of view. If, on the one hand, it is (1) a punishment of sin inflicted by the justice of God, on the other hand, it is (2) the especially appointed and only means of attaining true bliss, and of reaching the sublime end for which we have been created. Considered from the first point of view, it is quite right and proper that we should fear and dread its approach. But, considered from the second point of view, we should look forward to it as our friend and deliverer. As Rev. J. Nieremberg, S.J., so quaintly remarks:

'Death is a rare invention of God's mercy, for it easeth us of all molestations of this life, and takes away an eternity of miseries. Just consider what a painful thing it would be if we were for all eternity subject to the necessities of rising daily and of going to bed, of eating and drinking, of cold and heat, of toil and sickness, of seeking our sustenance, of carking and caring, of suffering affronts, or spending our whole life in sordid and laborious drudgery. Many that were notoriously wicked have sought death, and have made away with themselves, merely to avoid these inconveniences. At least, let us not dread this passage to a future felicity' ('Adoration in Spirit and Truth,' p. 378).

Indeed, 'death is so great a good, and so proper and secure an effect of God's goodness, that He would not leave it within the power of man's free will, or place it within the power of an enemy to hinder it. For, although it be *in anyone's power to deprive thee of life*, yet nobody, no, *not even the uncontrollable violence of kings, can deprive thee of death!* . . . Many, for a mere punctilio of worldly glory, have sought and coveted it; at least, for the glory of Heaven, let us not fear it' (p. 379). To the hardened sinner it is, of course, a fearful thing to fall into the hands of the living God. But to one who has always been solicitous about his salvation, and who is serving God loyally, nothing could be more desirable.

'As the love of God,' observes Père Grou, 'is their principal employment here, they see in the passage from this life only a happy change which will assure to them the possession of God, and the ineffable bliss of loving Him for all eternity. It is not that they have a positive assurance of their salvation, but they have a firm faith and trust in God, and their conscience bears witness to their constant fidelity to Him. . . . They know that it is Christ who will be their Judge, and they say to themselves: Why should I fear Him Who has given me so many graces, Who has preserved me from sin, or raised me up again, when I had fallen into it; Who inspired me with the desire of giving myself entirely to Him, Whom I love more than I love myself, and Whom I wish to love until my last breath?'*

To a soul in grace and free from all attachment to sin, what is death but the flinging open of his prison gates, the breaking of all earthly barriers, and the setting of the captive free? What indeed is death but the sweet voice of the heavenly Bridegroom, inviting His spouse, the redeemed and glorified soul, to the heavenly nuptials? When the cold sweat of death bedews the brow, and the last moments approach, and the ear grows insensible and closes to all earthly sounds, it will open to the soft, silvery echoes reaching it from another Land; and the departing soul will cry out in the hidden depths of its

* 'Manual for Interior Souls,' p. 246.

being: 'Behold, my Beloved speaketh to me: Arise, make haste, my love, my dove, my beautiful one, and COME. Winter (the winter of sin and of all spiritual bleakness and barrenness) is now past; the rain (the rain of trial, tribulation, and temptation) is over and gone; and the flowers (flowers of virtue and holiness) have appeared in the land. . . . My beloved to me, and I to Him, who feedeth among the lilies.'* Oh! who would wish to tarry a moment longer in this cold, dreary, dismal land of exile, when once the entrancing voice of the Beloved is heard calling him away to the inexpressible delights of Heaven, and to the 'nuptials of the Lamb'? Surely in an ecstasy of joy he will cry out: 'I have found Him, whom my soul loveth; I hold Him, and I will not let Him go.'†

Although no one has ever come back, to describe for us the sensations of passing from Time to Eternity, yet all the indications tend to show that there is no real pain. 'The pangs of birth are the mother's; the child, in all likelihood, does not suffer during its

* 'Canticle of Canticles,' chap. ii.

† *Ibid.*, iii. 4.

entry into the world, for its delicate organization could not survive such an ordeal. And so it is not unlikely that when the end comes, and we throw off life like a garment, *we too shall feel no pain.*'* Then, when we have passed the barrier, and pause, as it were, on the threshold of our new home, what will be our first sensations? On this subject, Cardinal Newman makes some apposite observations, which it may be interesting to quote.

'When,' observes the Cardinal, 'we have wound up our minds for any point of time, any great event, or interview with strangers, or the sight of some wonder, or the occasion of some unusual trial, when it comes, and is gone, we have a strange reverse of feeling from our changed circumstances. Such—but without any mixture of pain, without any lassitude, dullness, or disappointment—may be the happy contemplation of the disembodied spirit; as if it said to itself, "So now all is over; this is what I have so long waited for; for which I have nerved myself; against which I have prepared, fasted, prayed, and wrought

* 'The Adventure of Death,' p. 91.

righteousness. Death is come and gone—it is over. Ah! Is it possible? What an easy trial, what a cheap price for eternal glory! A few sharp sicknesses, or some acute pain awhile, or some few and evil years, or some struggles of mind, dreary desolateness for a season, fightings and fears, afflicting bereavements, or the scorn and ill usage of the world—how they fretted me, how much I thought of them, how little really they are! Oh, how contemptible a thing is human life—contemptible in itself, yet in its effect invaluable! For it has been to me like a small seed of easy purchase, germinating into bliss everlasting." '*

Pursuing much the same thought, but on a totally different occasion, the same Cardinal continues in the following strain:

'Blessed are they who shall at length behold what as yet mortal eye hath not seen and faith only enjoys. . . . Who can express the surprise and rapture which will come upon those who then at last apprehend them for the first time, and to whose perceptions they

* Newman's sermon on 'The Greatness and Littleness of Human Life,' p. 345.

are new? Who can imagine by a stretch of fancy the feelings of those who, having died in faith, wake up to enjoyment! The life then begun, we know, will last for ever; yet surely if memory be to us then what it is now, that will be a day much to be observed unto the Lord through all the ages of eternity. We may increase indeed for ever in knowledge and in love, still that first awaking from the dead, the day at once of our birth and our espousals, will ever be endeared and hallowed in our thoughts. When we find ourselves after a long rest gifted with fresh powers, vigorous with the seed of eternal life within us, able to love God as we wish, conscious that all trouble, sorrow, pain, anxiety, bereavement, is over for ever, blessed in the full affection of those earthly friends whom we loved so poorly, and could protect so feebly, while they were with us in the flesh, and above all, visited by the immediate visible ineffable Presence of Almighty God, with His Only-begotten Son our Lord Jesus Christ, and His Coequal, Coeternal Spirit, that great sight in which is the fullness of joy and pleasure for evermore—what deep, incommunicable, unimaginable thoughts will be then upon us! What depths will be stirred up within us! What secret harmonies awakened, of which human nature seemed incapable! Earthly words are indeed all worthless to minister to such high anticipations.'*

From the musing of Cardinal Newman we may pass to the following comforting words of another great Cardinal:

'In our eternal home there will be no distinctions of ranks, no divisions of classes of society,' writes Cardinal Wiseman, 'but all who have passed the threshold will be on a footing of equality in affection and charity. Is it possible, my God, that I shall one day be so highly honoured by those whom Thou hast so exalted? Shall Thy glorious Saints, shall Thy blessed Angels condescend to recognize and treat a poor wretch like me as a dear and long-tried friend, and as one worthy of their intimacy, familiarity, and love? . . . Reflect how the countless multitude of the Angels and Saints will be no impediment to this intercourse of charity. When we are introduced

* Newman's Sermon on 'The Invisible World,' pp. 229, 230.

to a great banquet on earth, our conversation is necessarily limited to the few individuals more immediately about us; we see the others only from a distance. But between spirits and spiritualized bodies, distance and multitude will be no hindrance to uninterrupted communion. They require not to be near one another in order to converse together: they have no need of individual friendships, or secret and reserved communications. We may form some idea of their intercourse by imagining them to ourselves as so many mirrors placed around the sun, which is God. Each of them reflects in itself the rays of all the others, and sends to them all its own images; and yet both the reflected and the reflector have only one object—viz., the sun—which gives them all light and heat, which multiplies itself as many fold as there are mirrors, and represents itself in each as many times as there are others that receive its figure. For what have the Blessed to say and express but what is in God, Who is all knowledge and wisdom, and Who, shining upon every one of His elect, makes in him the representation of Himself, in which he sees all that the others see, know, and feel, and by which he at once sends to and receives from them all faithful transcripts and representations of their common happiness? . . . The acquaintance and close friendship which we shall make with the Blessed will not be a work of time, or a feeling of gradual growth, but complete from the first instant. The very first moment of admission into their company will give the key to the thoughts and affections of all, and place each and all in the complete equality of communion. Oh, what a paradise of delights must Heaven be, where such an unimaginable participation of happiness is constantly carried on, where each one has nothing that is not the property of all, and where millions of souls contribute the sum of inconceivable bliss to form the portion of each!'*

'There is no better way of preparing for Eternity than by thinking of it and by keeping it ever before our minds. "The Saints tell us that one grand way of securing Heaven is to long for Heaven; and that, putting grievous sin out of the question, the reason why many souls have so long a Purgatory to undergo is

* *Vide* Cardinal Wiseman's 'Meditations,' pp. 306-7.

because they have not desired to look upon the Face of God" (p. 19).*

'Although I am always in perfect health,' writes Rev. J. P. Caussade, S.J., 'I feel that the years, so rapidly passing, will *soon* bring me to that eternal goal to which we are all hastening. True! This thought is bitter to nature, but by dint of considering it as salutary, it becomes almost agreeable, as a disgusting remedy gradually ceases to appear so when its good effects have been experienced. One of my friends said, the other day, that in getting old it seemed to him time passed with increasing rapidity, and that weeks seemed to him as short as days used to be, months like weeks, and years like months. As to that, what do a few years more or less signify to us, who have to live and continue as long as God Himself? Those who have gone before us twenty or thirty years ago, or even a century, or those who will follow us twenty or thirty years hence, will neither be behindhand nor before others in that vast Eternity; but it will seem to all of us as though we

* From a sermon preached by Bp. Hedley, March 12, 1893, at Warrington.

began it together. Oh, what power does not this thought contain to soften the rigours of our short and miserable life, which, patiently endured, will be to our advantage. A longer or a shorter life, a little more or a little less pain, what is it in comparison with the eternal life that awaits us ? towards which we are approaching rapidly, incessantly, and which is almost in sight, for me especially, who am, as it were, on the brink, and on the point of embarking.'*

The supernal joys and delights of our heavenly Home have been depicted again and again by gifted and saintly writers. And although these entrancing word-pictures, which have been painted for our delectation, often possess a depth of beauty that ravishes the mind and sets the heart on fire, and although their contemplation is exceedingly useful and stimulating, and well calculated to stir us up and to instil a strong and insatiable longing in our hearts, yet we must ever bear in mind that even the very best and choicest of these descriptions falls infinitely short of the transcendent truth. The

* See 'Abandonment to Divine Providence,' pp. 176-7.

most sublime and exquisite representations that can be set before us, in the most eloquent and glowing language, to excite our thirst and to arouse our desires, are, after all, nothing better than a rude and clumsy sketch of the tremendous reality. Not one of these conceptions, however beautiful, ever sins by excess, but every one of them sins, and sins grievously, by defect. For we know full well that when the utmost has been said it has not drawn anywhere near the full truth, and that even the wisest and the holiest, in attempting the fruitless task, does but stammer and mutter like a little child in its first attempts to articulate.

Yet if even such hopelessly inadequate attempts are so powerful to awaken desire and to inflame the affections, what—let us ask ourselves—must be the effect of the unapproachable and infinite reality, when at last it actually bursts upon us in all its inconceivable beauty and perfection! God grant that, on that eventful day, we may find ourselves among the elect, and that we may not then see the bright vision vanishing for ever from before our eyes, and the gates of hell opening to receive us instead. Yet it rests with ourselves. 'BEFORE MAN IS LIFE AND DEATH: GOOD AND EVIL: THAT WHICH HE SHALL CHOOSE SHALL BE GIVEN TO HIM.'* Oh, what a responsibility rests upon our poor weak shoulders!

'Unam petii a Domino, hanc requiram; ut inhabitem in domo Domini omnibus diebus vitae meae.'†

We will conclude this chapter with a quotation from St. Gregory and another from Bishop Hedley:

'Stir up your hearts; enkindle your faith; and long with ardent aspirations for the Heaven above. *To long for Heaven is to travel to Heaven.* Let no difficulty hold you back; let desire smooth the roughest way. Turn not aside to the pleasant places of this fleeting world. Fix not your hearts on the things that you must one day leave behind. You are the sheep of a heavenly Shepherd, and His pastures are above; and it is to your heavenly country that you must lift your hearts.'‡

* Ecclus. xv. 18. † Ps. xxvi.

‡ Words of St. Gregory the Great, quoted by Bishop Hedley.

Bear in mind that 'whatever raises the heart above the distracting and engrossing scenes of earth—above the common and poor elements of our daily life—makes for the advantage and the happiness of men. For it is for the future that we are made; and to keep the eye upon the future, and to restrain the affections from the present, this is our human end and purpose; and if it is what we are made for, IT IS WHAT WE SHOULD GLORY IN.'*

* Bishop Hedley, *Idem*, p. 1.

## CHAPTER VII

## REJOICE AND BE GLAD

Vital spark of heavenly flame!
Quit, oh, quit this mortal frame!
Trembling, hoping, ling'ring, flying,
Oh, the pain, the BLISS of dying!
Cease, fond nature, cease thy strife,
And let me languish into life!

Hark! They whisper; angels say,
'Sister spirit, come away!'
What is this absorbs me quite?
Steals my senses, shuts my sight,
Drowns my spirit, draws my breath?
Tell me, my soul, can this be death?

POPE.

SOME good men are inclined to discourage the thought of Heaven and the contemplation of its joys. They tell us that God should be served and loved for His own sake, and not for the sake of His rewards, and that we should all do our duty because it is our duty, and altogether irrespective of consequences. In short, they would persuade us that it is *selfish* to attach importance to the rewards of our actions, and wholly unworthy of a generous soul.

Thus, for instance, Père Grou, S.J., writes: 'So long as we love God with some thought of our own advantage remaining—as long as we seek our own interest in His service—as long as we seek ourselves ever so little—as long as we strive after perfection for our own sakes, and for the spiritual good that it will bring us—in a word, as long as the human "I" enters into our intentions, so long will that intention be, I will not say criminal or even bad, but mixed up with imperfection and impurity.'* But whence arises this imperfection of motive here spoken of? Fortunately the late Bishop Hedley, O.S.B., supplies us with a ready answer. In his 'Retreat' (p. 399) he writes: 'The imperfection of this motive arises when we separate the thought of bliss from the thought of God.' But this, of course, should never be done! The Bishop then goes on to explain that 'the true view is that God's possession, and perfect bliss, are one and the same thing. . . . The thought of our future rewards is a useful

* *Vide* 'Manual for Interior Souls,' p. 228.

thought and true, as far as it goes; but *to remove its imperfection,* we should accustom ourselves to reflect that God Himself is our reward.' Regarded from that point of view, which is the only really correct one, he strongly recommends the consideration of our future happiness, as an excellent motive. He writes: 'It is a useful thought and true. To aim at celestial happiness is to live for God and for God alone, and whilst the Christian in this life tramples *self* underfoot, in order to give himself wholly to his God, even in the bliss of the other world he will be absorbed in God, and will find his happiness in that very absorption. If this is selfishness (he exclaims) it is of the very essence of nature, and the most imperative command of grace.'*

The Rev. J. P. de Caussade, S.J., writing to a certain nun, Sister Charlotte-Elizabeth Bourcier de Monthureux, in 1734, also says something very much to the purpose, so I will make no apology for quoting him also:

'I much approve of the reply you made to the person who told you that she did not love God with sufficient disinterestedness.

* 'Retreat,' p. 400.

This is a visible *illusion of the devil*, who, under pretext of I know not what self-love, wants to keep this soul back, and to retard its progress. Tell her that self-love (I allude to spiritual self-love, which, although not sinful, tarnishes the perfect purity of Divine love) is only found in those souls who make of the gifts of God, or of His rewards, a motive to love Him for the sake of these gifts. . . . To love God for Himself and because He is God, and in as much as He is our own God, our GREAT REWARD, our sovereign good, infinitely good to us, is the pure and practical love of the saints. FOR TO LOVE ONE'S SUPREME HAPPINESS, WHICH IS GOD HIMSELF, IS TO LOVE GOD ALONE. These two terms express the same thing, and it is impossible to love God otherwise than as He is in Himself. Besides, in Himself He is our supreme good, our last end, and our eternal happiness.

'But someone will say: Supposing that God were not our eternal happiness, ought we not to love Him just the same, for Himself? Oh, what a strange and pitiable supposition! It is as much as to say, If God were not God! Do not let us split hairs so much, but go on in a direct and simple manner, broad-mindedly, as St. Francis of Sales advises. Let us love God with simplicity and as well as we can, and He will raise and purify our love even more and more according to His own good pleasure.'*

Dr. Mozley also refers to this subject, in one of his 'University Sermons,' and though he is not a Catholic, his words are worth recording, as an appeal to common sense:

'We would ask of one who argues against the desire of Heaven, as being a SELFISH motive—When you come to the *actual* in man, can you deny that there is something excellent and lofty in his pursuing the good of a distant and supernatural sphere, from which he is divided by a whole gulf of being? Can you help yourself recognizing a nobility in thus reaching forward towards the happiness of an unseen world at the sacrifice of the present, even though it *is* his own happiness that he aims at? Is it not something which you cannot help morally admiring, though it is for himself that he wishes? And if so, is not your argument from *self* gone?' (p. 66).

* *Vide* 'Abandonment to Divine Providence,' p. 370.

He further observes that 'the Christian hope of immortality cannot be an egotistic hope, because the affection does not centre upon an individual; it is in its very essence social; love enters into its very composition, and it looks forward to a communion of good as its very end and goal.'*

All spiritual writers readily admit that the hope of Heaven is a far higher and nobler motive than the fear of hell. All allow that the desire of reward, especially when the reward consists in the possession of God, is a stimulus better than, and superior to, the dread of punishment. If, then, the thought of the appalling torments prepared by God for those who offend Him is a useful, a salutary, and a thoroughly commendable motive, and one strongly recommended by even the greatest saints, surely we need have no scruples in recommending the thought of the inconceivable delights which God has prepared for those who love Him. In many a startling passage in Holy Writ we are commanded to dread the awful judgments of God. 'Fear not them that kill the body, and are not able to kill the

* 'University Sermons,' p. 70.

soul; but rather fear Him, who can cast both soul and body into hell' (Matt. x. 28). In order to inspire the hearts of his hearers with this salutary fear the prophet Isaias puts them these searching questions: 'Which of you can dwell with devouring fire? Which of you shall dwell with everlasting burnings?' (xxxiii. 14). Many—perhaps the great majority of men—are restrained and kept from sin by the fear of hell. And saints and doctors of the Church and preachers and missioners and retreat-givers and others are never weary of describing the torments of the damned, and the horrors of their surroundings. If, then, the thought of hell be encouraged, and made use of, and approved of, surely we need have no hesitation in making frequent use of the higher and far nobler thought of Heaven.

Did any lingering doubt remain lurking in our mind, the example of our Divine Lord Himself would instantly drive it away. He frequently cheered His hearers by reminding them of the glorious future in store for them. He evidently wishes His followers to think of Heaven, and to encourage themselves by such reflections, and to feel happy at the prospect before them. Else, indeed, why should He cry out: '*Be glad and rejoice, for your reward is very great in Heaven*'? (Matt. v. 12). Why should He exhort them saying: '*Rejoice in this, that your names are written in Heaven*'? (Luke x. 20). For how can we continue to rejoice and to be glad, unless we continue to think of our good fortune, and of all the delights which our heavenly Father has in reserve for His children? Jesus Christ even urges us to exert ourselves and to make every effort to increase this reward still further. As, for instance, where He bids us to 'lay up to ourselves treasures in Heaven, where neither rust nor moth doth consume, and where thieves do not break through, nor steal' (Matt. vi. 20). Surely, if God incarnate *tells us to be glad and to rejoice* because of the bright Home above, into which He desires to welcome us one day, and if He even urges us to render it still more beautiful and glorious by our good works and the exercise of charity, we should try and do what He tells us, and love to occupy ourselves constantly with the thought of His immense generosity and liberality and love.

This, at all events, seems to be the view which the Saints took of the matter, and they are our great models and most precious examples. Just consider, for instance, the glorious St. Paul, one of the greatest and most generous-hearted of the Saints. Did he not rejoice, as he was bidden, at the thought of Heaven? Who can listen, in imagination, to his words, and not feel his emotion of triumph and of exultation and joy, as he breaks forth: 'The time of my dissolution is at hand; I have fought a good fight; I have finished my course; I have kept the faith. As to the rest, THERE IS LAID UP FOR ME A CROWN OF JUSTICE, WHICH THE LORD, THE JUST JUDGE, WILL TENDER TO ME IN THAT DAY' (2 Tim. iv. 7).

Or listen to holy David crying out in wonder and delight, 'Oh, how lovely are Thy tabernacles, O Lord of hosts. My soul longeth and fainteth for the courts of the Lord' (Ps. lxxxiii. 1). So again: 'As the hart panteth after the fountains of water, so my soul panteth after Thee, O God' (Ps. xli.). 'When shall I come and appear before the face of God?' The same longing and feeling of impatience is found in other saints. 'Ah, when shall I see death,' demands St. Leonard; 'when shall I see these bonds, which bind me to earth, broken? When will that happy moment come, when I shall behold my God?' When St. Paul of the Cross was lying sick, he cried out in great joy: 'My prison walls are falling, and the poor prisoner will soon fly away to the glorious liberty of the children of God.' St. Francis of Sales, in his last illness, we are told, felt a particular delight in repeating: 'My heart and my flesh rejoice in the living God. When shall I appear before His face?' Blessed Colomba, in her last sickness, was heard to exclaim with much earnestness: 'O Death, precious in the sight of God, come and delay no longer, since every delay is a torment to me. Come, my only comfort, for thou alone canst eternally unite me to my sweet Spouse.'

But we might fill a volume with similar instances. But *cui bono?* Let us rather listen to St. Francis of Sales, who tells us that 'a heart burning with divine love, feeling that during its pilgrimage here below it will never be able to glorify God or hear Him worthily praised by others, longs to burst the bonds which link it to the earth, and to soar to the regions where He is perfectly glorified. This continually increasing desire,' continues the Saint, 'sometimes acquires so great an ascendancy over the soul, that it banishes every other wish, and inspires her with a mortal disgust for the things of earth; she then endures a languor and debility which leads her to the brink of the grave; *and it sometimes happens that she actually expires, when God permits this desire to become extreme.*'*

It is generally taught that Our Blessed Lady died from the very vehemence of her love.†

That the Church approves and even encourages this thirst and this longing for the delights of Heaven is clearly shown by her universal practice. She teaches us to pray that we may secure these joys, and puts words of the greatest longing into our mouths. Not only in the 'Our Father' does she bid

* See Pagani, 'Science of the Saints,' vol. iii., p. 574.

† 'Saepe amor potest esse tam vehemens, ut sequatur mors, omni spiritu vitali, prae nimia cordis dilatatione, diffluente. Sic multi putant B. Virginem vi amoris mortuam.' (*Vide* Lessius, 'De Nominibus Dei,' p. 212.)

us ask a hundred times a day that God's glorious Kingdom may come, but in the Holy Mass, in the Divine Office, in her liturgical prayers, she seems never to be weary of urging us to aspire after the happiness and the joys of our Home above.

Priests are expected to turn their thoughts heavenwards *even before the Mass begins*, and while they are vesting. Both Bishop and priest, while putting on the amice, are instructed to say: 'Make me white, O Lord, and cleanse my heart, that, whitened in the Blood of the Lamb, I may possess *eternal joys*.' While adjusting the maniple, the Bishop prays that he may so carry it, '*ut cum exsultatione recipiam mercedem laboris*,' and the priest in like manner. So, again, on taking the stole, both Bishop and priest end the prescribed prayer with: 'Though unworthy I approach Thy Sacred Mysteries, yet may I merit everlasting joys.'

This '*gaudium sempiternum*,' or everlasting joy, is never lost sight of. So, during the course of the Mass, the celebrant humbly begs God to vouchsafe to grant him '*some part and fellowship with His holy apostles and martyrs; with John, Stephen, Matthias, Barnabas,'* and the rest, '*intra quorum nos consortium, non aestimator meriti, sed veniae, quaesumus, largitor admitte.*' A little later, while placing the particle into the chalice, he prays that '*Haec commixtio . . . fiat accipientibus in* VITAM AETERNAM.'

So, again, when reciting the Preface, in Masses for the Dead, he renders thanks to the 'Almighty Father, everlasting God, through Christ our Lord, *in whom the hope of a blessed resurrection is shown to us, that they who are saddened by the certain necessity of dying be comforted by the promise of eternal life to come. For the life of Thy faithful, O Lord, is changed, not destroyed; and when the home of this earthly life is dissolved, an everlasting dwelling in Heaven shall be gained. Wherefore, with Angels and Archangels, with the Thrones and Dominions, etc., we sing,*' and so forth.

It is said that St. Teresa could hardly listen to the *Credo* without falling into an ecstasy. Her soul was full to overflowing with the highest and most vivid conceptions of the splendour and magnificence of the heavenly places, so that when she heard the words, 'cujus regni non erit finis' (*Whose Kingdom shall have no end*), she frequently fainted away.

Should the celebrant make use of the beautiful prayers after Mass, provided in most Missals, he will find himself again invited to implore God to grant him a place among the Saints and Angels of Heaven. The first is composed by St. Thomas, and ends as follows: '*Et precor Te, ut ad illud ineffabile convivium me peccatorem perducere digneris; ubi Tu cum Filio Tuo, et Spiritu Sancto, Sanctis Tuis es lux vera, satietas plena, gaudium sempiternum, jucunditas consummata, et felicitas perfecta.*' The next prayer is by another great saint—viz., St. Bonaventure. He, in like manner, is athirst for the crown, promised to all who have 'fought the good fight,' and implores God '*ut langueat et liquefiat anima mea solo semper amore et desiderio Tui, Te concupiscat, et deficiat in atria Tua, cupiat dissolvi, et esse Tecum,*' etc. Upon this follows the Rhythmus of St. Thomas, 'Adoro Te devote latens Deitas,' which ends also with a great sigh for the heavenly country:

Jesu, quem velatum nunc aspicio,
Oro fiat illud, *quod tam sitio ;*
Ut Te revelata cernens facie,
Visu sim beatus Tuae gloriae. Amen.

Even the well-known prayer beginning 'Anima Christi sanctifica me' winds up in the same way: '*Jube me venire ad Te, ut cum Sanctis Tuis laudem Te in saecula saeculorum.*'

We have referred to the prayers which form a part of *every* Mass, but even the *special* prayers, which differ according to the season of the year and according to the particular saint commemorated, very frequently renew the same petition, and sometimes more than once during the same Mass. If, for example, we turn to the Mass for Thursday in Holy Week, we find the priest asking for '*everlasting bliss*' and for '*everlasting joys*' both in the Secret and again in the Post-Communion.

If we examine the prayers composed by the Church, in honour of her innumerable saints, which we are obliged to say both in the Mass and in the Divine Office, we shall be surprised to note how often she directs our thoughts to our heavenly country. How many terminate in some such form as this:

'Grant, through his merits and intercession, that we may be worthy to win our *heavenly country*' (St. Titus); or, 'Grant through his intercession that we may be loosed from the bonds of sin, and enjoy freedom for evermore in *our heavenly kingdom*' (St. Peter Nolasco); or, 'Grant that, by the help and merits of St. Scholastica, we may live in such innocence as to be worthy to win *bliss everlasting*' (St. Scholastica); or, 'Grant, we beseech Thee, that we may faithfully follow what he preached and taught, and may thus win the glory of *everlasting light*' (St. Kentigern); or, 'Give us grace, we beseech Thee, to honour him upon earth, that we may be able to *reign with him in heaven*' (St. Ethelbert); or, 'Grant that, with his help and by his example, we may so fight on earth as to become worthy to be *crowned with him in heaven*' (St. Ignatius); or, 'Give us grace to think lightly of the pleasures of this world, and to gain a throne of glory with her for evermore' (St. Winefride). These are but a few specimens of the endings of the prayers which the Church, in her wisdom, prescribes to be said at Mass and in the Divine Office, but they sufficiently indicate her mind and reveal her desire that we should keep the idea of future bliss ever before us.

Every time we recite Matins we beg for a share in the joys of the future life, both before the Fourth Lesson and before the last. In the first case we ask that '*Christus perpetuae det nobis gaudia vitae*'; and, in the second place, that '*Ad societatem civium supernorum perducat nos Rex Angelorum.*'

Nor is this all. We are sometimes actually instructed to ask the Saints to obtain for us from God a more vehement desire for His heavenly kingdom. Thus, for example, on the feast of St. Edmund (November 16), 'ad utrasque Vesp. et ad Laudes,' the cantor sings: '*Nobis in hoc exsilio, Sancte Pater Edmunde,*' and the choir replies: 'COELESTIS PATRIAE AMOREM, *quaesumus infunde.*'

These are but a few specimens of hundreds of similar petitions, all of which suggest a high appreciation and a fervent longing for the joys of Heaven and the society of the Saints and Angels. In this way the Church seems to wish to lift up our thoughts and to fill our hearts with eager desires after God and all that the possession of God really means.

The world is dark and there is so much to sadden and to depress us that she would lighten our darkness, and cheer us amid our sorrows, by directing our attention to that peace which surpasseth all understanding, to that joy which no words can express, and to that happiness which no mind can conceive, but which God has promised to those who serve and love Him.

As the labourer in the midst of his wearisome toil cheers himself up by thoughts of the wages awaiting him, and the rest and peace which will be his when his heavy task is done, so will the faithful servant of God wisely and rightly encourage and lighten the burden of life, by calling to mind the inconceivably rich promises and the undreamed-of rewards which His Divine Master has promised him, when he has accomplished the task that He, in His providence, has given him to do.

Even St. Peter himself did not hesitate to inquire what recompense he was to receive for having left 'all things' to follow our Blessed Lord. 'Quid erit nobis?' And, what is yet more worthy of note, Our Lord did not tell him that, having done a noble act, he should rest content, and not concern himself about the reward. On the contrary, He answered: 'You, who have followed Me, . . . when the Son of Man shall sit on the seat of His Majesty, you also shall sit on twelve seats, judging the twelve tribes of Israel,' thereby evidently wishing to encourage him. But He did more. He made a magnificent promise not only to the Apostles, but to all who in future ages should imitate the Apostles and leave their possessions to devote themselves to His service. '*Every one* who hath left house or brethren or sisters or father or mother or wife or children or lands for My name's sake, shall receive a hundredfold, and shall possess life everlasting' (Matt. xix. 29).

Was no attention to be paid to this promise? Was all thought of the recompense to be forgotten and set deliberately aside as unworthy of a true lover of Christ? Such a view is unthinkable. The splendid promise was made on purpose to stimulate and to encourage, and to draw many hearts to make the sacrifice. Since those Divine words were spoken, they have rung in the ears of millions and stirred countless hearts, and have led thousands, yea, hundreds of thousands, to join the ranks of the priesthood, and to enter upon the religious life. In plain truth, the promise was set forth as a motive; it was offered as an inducement; it was intended as an argument addressed to (not selfish, but) generous and devoted minds; and its effect, during all the long centuries of the Church's history, has been immense and quite marvellous. We are human; and God, who knows the clay out of which we are formed, is well aware that we are strongly influenced by the prospect of rewards; and every fervent Catholic is as ready to acknowledge that fact to-day, as holy David was thousands of years ago, when he exclaimed: '*I have inclined my heart to do Thy justifications for ever,* FOR THE SAKE OF THE REWARD' (Ps. cxviii. 112). When we consider that the very essence of this reward is nothing less than God Himself, we shall realize that to labour and to suffer and to spend ourselves for the sake of the reward is really to labour and to suffer and to spend ourselves for the sake of God, Whom we love above all things, and Whom we desire to please, and with Whom we long most intensely to be united.

There is no doubt but that the Saints found strength and comfort in the thought of eternal happiness; then why should not we? In times of trial and danger they were sustained and buoyed up and rendered capable of enduring even the most appalling tortures, by fixing their gaze upon the splendour and the magnificence of the reward. The Saints and Martyrs, especially in the first ages of the Church, embraced all kinds of trials and torments, not only with patience and resignation to the will of God, but also with transports of joy, because they were convinced that what they suffered bore no proportion to the incomprehensible joys reserved in Heaven for the faithful servants of God; according to the words of the Apostle: '*The sufferings of this present time are not worthy to be compared with the glory that is to be revealed hereafter,* for a moment of light tribulation *worketh for us, above measure exceedingly, an eternal weight of glory*' (2 Cor. iv. 17). To object to the thought of Heaven, as encouraging selfishness, and as indicating a want of true love of God, is surely to go too far. It would not only look like criticizing Our Lord, Who distinctly bids us '*rejoice and be glad,*' but it would deprive us of one of the most powerful motives we have for serving Him. As Pagani very truly observes: 'The hope of receiving so ample a recompense sweetened all the sufferings and afflictions of the holy martyrs, and bathed their souls in a torrent of delights, even whilst their bodies streamed with blood, and smarted under stripes that were inflicted by their cruel tormentors' (p. 221). Indeed, the thought of this recompense is an excellent one, and recommended by no less an authority than St. Paul, who, writing to the Corinthians, says: '*Every one that striveth for the mastery refraineth himself from all things; and they indeed that they may receive a corruptible crown; but we an* INCORRUPTIBLE ONE' (ix. 25).

The great Apostle evidently approves of this motive, and encourages it, by his apostolic authority. When, indeed, we consider how many there are ready to strive and to deny themselves, and to lead laborious lives, for the sake of the very poor and unsatisfying prizes of this world, we can well understand what a strong and powerful incentive an eternal and an incorruptible crown in Heaven must be.

We have an excellent illustration of this in the case of a certain Fra Domenico, a famous hermit, whose wonderful career is referred to in ‘The Life of St. Catherine de Ricci’:

‘Domenico, we are told by Sandrini, was a simple and unlearned man, but with such an upright soul that he made immense progress in the science of prayer and the love of God, and gained large profit from paying yearly visits to St. Catherine, whom he called his mother. One year Catherine had given him, as a particular practice, never to lose sight of Heaven, and of the joy and glory that he hoped for there as his reward. The holy man took his staff and wallet, and started afresh on his peregrinations from town to town, and shrine to shrine; and at every step he took, at every alms he asked, and at every prayer he said, in all his annoyances and all his penances, he thought, as he had been told, of Heaven, with its joys and glories; and behold! this sweet thought lessened his burdens, scattered his cares, and soothed his weariness. Then, comparing the little that he did for God with the great things that God was preparing for him, he blushed to be such a cowardly servant, and so niggardly of his services to such a great and munificent Lord. Thereupon he redoubled his prayers, fasts, penances, and good works, and patience under trial; in short, his fervour in everything. But do as he would, the vision of Heaven constantly grew before his mind's eye, bringing with it a *perfect torrent of inward joy*, so that, as he increased his labours, he did but increase his happiness, and there were times when he even fell by the way, as he journeyed, actually overcome by the greatness of his delight. Had anyone, at such moments, met the poor begging hermit, covered with sweat and dust, and gasping for breath, beneath some tree or hedge, he must have been filled with pity for his apparently wretched state of want and fatigue. Yet, this man was *just then happier than a king on his throne*, inwardly revelling in joys unknown to the ordinary mortal. When the year had run out, the disciple went back to St. Catherine for a fresh lesson. She suggested no new practice, but recommended him to keep always to the same, no other having been so sweet and fruitful. . . . It used to be said, in the Convent, that when this holy mother (Catherine) and son discoursed of the future life and its mysteries, wonderful things passed between them. . . . They are said to have been rapt sometimes, when together, into extraordinary ecstasies.'*

Would it not be well for us to follow the splendid example of this simple hermit? Should we not be far happier, as well as far holier, if we kept the thought of God's supernatural gifts before our minds, and adopted the method of Fra Domenico, so highly recommended by such a glorious saint as St. Catherine and so successful in its results? Look around upon the world to-day. On every side we see immense numbers of ambitious men and women, labouring and toiling and enduring every sort of hardship, privation, and fatigue, in order to gain some purely earthly and temporal end, upon which they

* *Vide* 'St. Catherine de Ricci,' by F. M. Capes, pp. 224, 225.

have set their hearts. Surely, we ought to be prepared to do as much, and indeed infinitely more, for the sake of what is not only heavenly, but everlasting.

There can be no doubt but that we do not make sufficient use of 'the glory to come' as a motive. Though many beautiful works have been composed and published to help us in our struggles after holiness and perfection, yet how very few lay any great stress on this motive, which is one of the most attractive of all. Take, for instance, such an admirable and at the same time such a very practical and well-known book as 'Meditations on the Principal Truths of Religion,' by the Most Rev. Dr. Kirby, Archbishop of Ephesus, a favourite book with many of the clergy. There is scarcely a paragraph about Heaven and its entrancing joys in any one of its pages.* Yet there are no less than four entire meditations on hell and its torments, occupying some fifty or sixty full pages. Surely Heaven is quite as much 'one of the

* See the Preface, p. ix, where I am able to quote just a sentence or two concerning Heaven from this book, but they are the only examples I could find.

*principal Truths of Religion* ' as hell, yet it is set aside and passed over. The same observations may be made in regard to many other books, which are put into the hands of both clergy and lay-folk, such as the 'Exercitia Spiritualia S.P. Ignatii Loyolae' ('The Spiritual Exercises of Saint Ignatius'). This is one of the best known and one of the most famous books of the kind in the world, yet the pious reader will not find a single page about the delights of Heaven, though he may search from cover to cover. Little or nothing is made of the ' Crown of Eternal Glory ' awaiting the faithful soul, so soon as his course has run. What is the consequence ? The consequence is that while the man of the world is all on fire in his anxiety to win his *corruptible crown*, the zealous man of God scarcely troubles himself to think at all of the *incorruptible crown that is offered him by God.* Thus one of the most powerful motives is shamefully neglected !

## CHAPTER VIII

## STEPS ON THE GOLDEN STAIRS

Out of the shadows of sadness
Into the sunshine of gladness,
Into the light of the blest;
Out of a land very dreary,
Into the rapture of rest.

*     *     *     *     *

Into a joyland above us,
Where there's a Father to love us—
Into our Home—Sweet Home.

FATHER RYAN.

IT has often been said—and there seems no reason to doubt the statement—that if we could carry off even the very worst and most hardened and inveterate sinner, and place him for a while on the brink of the bottomless pit of hell, and let him see for himself, and with his own eyes, all the unspeakable horrors and all the excruciating torments reserved for criminals like himself, he would be so absolutely terrified and so deeply moved and alarmed at the sight, that he would instantly change his evil ways, give up sin, and begin to lead the life of a saint. One glimpse of hell would so burn itself into his memory, that it would never be forgotten.*

The thought of those lurid fires would haunt him night and day; the distorted limbs of the damned, writhing under their eternal tortures, would be ever before his eyes; the crackling of the flames, the gnashing of teeth, and the piercing shrieks and deafening yells of agony ever in his ears. He would start and tremble at the bare shadow of sin whenever it crossed his path, and would fly from temptation as from the face of a fiery serpent. In fact, he would spend the rest of his days in the exercise of heroic virtue. And, observe, he would be moved to do this, not because of any

* St. Teresa was once granted a vision of hell, and it haunted her for years. Fully six years after the terrific experience she wrote, as follows, to a friend: 'I was terrified by that vision, and that *terror is on me even now while I am writing;* and though it took place six years ago, the natural warmth of my body is chilled by fear even now. And so, amid all the pain and suffering which I may have had to bear, I remember no time in which I do not think that, by comparison, all we have to suffer in this world is as nothing. It seems to me that we complain without reason' (*vide* 'Life,' written by herself, chap. xxxii., p. 267).

new truth that had been revealed to him, but solely because he had been brought to realize and to understand, for the first time, all the horrors and frightful meanings of *an old truth, familiar to him from childhood*—namely, that hell itself is awaiting the impenitent sinner, to torment him, in inextinguishable fires, for ever and ever. For to believe is one thing, but to realize is quite another. And hell realized is a most powerful and almost irresistible motive.

This is, no doubt, true. But, after all, man is so constituted that he is found to be just as strongly attracted by rewards as he is repelled by punishments, and perhaps even more so. The experience of past ages proves that even the poor and unworthy pleasures of this earth allure him to destruction, quite as effectually as the candle allures the moth. Just think of the millions and millions who give way to sins of the flesh; millions and millions who deliberately run the risk of eternal damnation, the loss of Heaven, and the friendship and love of God Himself, for the sake of the enjoyment, the *momentary* enjoyment, of a gross forbidden pleasure.

Oh, if the weak and sordid pleasures of this world hold such a despotic sway, and exert such a tremendous influence over men, what would be the strength and the influence of the exquisite delights of Heaven, if only they could be realized ? There are many things that lead men to commit sin, but it is the strong thirst for pleasure, rather than for anything else, that possesses this awful power. We have just referred, as an example, to sins of the flesh. Pause for a moment and reflect that in this case, though men are invited to break the Law of God, yet they are offered nothing substantial, nothing of permanent value, in return. No; nothing more than a little sensual sensation, which can be enjoyed but for a moment. Yet, even that attracts them, as the magnet attracts steel. They will seek this indulgence with the greatest assiduity, nor do they care what extravagant price they pay for it. Thousands have ruined their health, sacrificed their reputation, lost good situations, and faced disgrace rather than deny themselves even the lowest animal pleasure, once placed within their reach. Nay, more, many, as though rendered desperate and reckless and maddened by the very vehemence of their desire, have turned their backs upon God Himself, forfeited Heaven, and have braved the eternal torments of hell, *to which they knew they were exposing themselves,* rather than forgo the low and shameful gratification of a moment.

Other temptations attract men by offering them a great variety of different things, but things, at least, of some reputed value, such as wealth, position, success in business, the removal of a rival, the death of an enemy, and so forth; but sins of the flesh have nothing to offer but a momentary sensual gratification; a brief sensible delight. Yet this notwithstanding, the prospect of this miserable and sordid pleasure is found to exercise a far more powerful influence over men than the prospect of higher and much more substantial gains. The fact is, that men are more allured by pleasure, poor though it may be, and are more readily won over and captivated by it, than by anything else which other temptations have to offer as the reward of disobedience.

Alas! it is but too well known that so strong is its attraction, and so deadly is its fascination, that more are drawn down to hell *by this one sin,* not merely than by any other, but, *terribile dictu,* than by *all other sins put together.* This was the deliberate opinion of such a wise and such an experienced old saint as St. Alphonsus, and is the common opinion of most spiritual writers of to-day.*

Now, my argument is this: If base and degrading and purely earthly pleasures such as these can and do actually exercise so extraordinary a power over men, surely the thought, and still more the well-founded hope, of the immeasurably higher and intenser and more gratifying and enduring pleasures of Heaven should not only quench all sinful lust for earthly pleasures, and dull their attraction, but should fill every thoughtful man with disgust and horror for earthly joys

* Speaking of the Sixth and the Ninth Commandments, St. Alphonsus introduces the subject in the following terrible words: '*Utinam brevius aut obscurius explicare me potuissem. Sed cum sit frequentior ac abundantior confessionum materia* et propter quam major animarum numerus ad infernum dilabitur, imo non dubito asserere ob hoc unum impudicitiae vitium, aut saltem non sine eo, omnes damnari quicumque damnantur,' etc. (*vide* 'Theologica'; Tractus de sexto et nono Decalogi Praecepto, p. 215).

and with an immense appreciation of heavenly ones, together with an insatiable desire for their attainment. Hence, Heaven assiduously contemplated, Heaven thoughtfully considered and meditated, should prove a most powerful and almost irresistible stimulus. Its sounds and scenes, so infinitely superior to any to be met with on earth, its peace and rest and perfect tranquillity, its beauty and splendour and loveliness, so far surpassing even our wildest dreams; the society of Angels and Saints, and of the three Persons of the Blessed Trinity, and the complete absence of all that could molest, or disturb, or trouble the heart or mind, together with the most perfect satisfaction of every sense of the body and of every power of the soul, would draw our hearts as nothing else ever could, and would excite within them a thirst that nothing else could satisfy. And the more the mind dwelt upon these infinite joys and delights, and the more it familiarized itself with them, the more intense and the more irresistible would become the hunger and the thirst for Heaven and all that Heaven means. The whole soul would yearn, with an incredible impatience, for the 'courts of the Lord.' It would desire them before all things, and would cheerfully pay any price and accept any condition, so that it might one day really come to enjoy such an entrancingly happy existence.

However, in order that the thought of Heaven should produce its full effect upon me, and prove a really powerful motive, four conditions are essential. In the *first* place, I must realize, in some measure, the magnitude of the reward that is offered, and fully persuade myself that it exceeds, in an immeasurable degree, anything that eye has ever seen, or ear has ever heard, or intellect ever conceived. In the *second* place, I must fully acknowledge and thoroughly convince myself that this reward is prepared, and is destined *for me.* And in the *third place,* I must clearly understand and bring home to myself that this tremendous and wholly unspeakable treasure is placed, in very truth, actually within my reach, and that it not only *may,* but that it most undoubtedly *will, be mine,* if only I love God and keep His commandments. In the *fourth* place, I must live my daily life in the full consciousness that I am ever hastening towards this great object of my desire, day by day, and without a single moment's cessation, and that each hour and each moment is really bringing me a step nearer to this Home of supreme and infinite joy, and furthermore that it is possible even that I may be called, at any unexpected moment, to enter into 'the joy of the Lord.'

If these four conditions are ever present before the mind, and if they are allowed to exert their full influence on the soul, they will produce a wonderful change in any individual, however he may be circumstanced. They will set him furiously thinking, planning, and arranging so as to render his possession of the heavenly prize as secure as possible. They will so draw his affections towards the Goal, that he will be prepared to suffer anything and to do anything in order to reach it. They will so arouse his desires, that he will most willingly and most readily follow the narrow way, and the straight path, that leads to Heaven, and would be ready to do so with equal earnestness, even were it a thousand times harder and more painful than it really is. In fact, with his exalted conception of the delights of Heaven, he would consider these delights very cheaply won *at any price whatsoever*. But, when he realizes how exceedingly little is really demanded of him, and how, in sober truth, God offers Him His heavenly Kingdom (and all that is involved in the term) for doing merely his duty, he makes up his mind, with the firmest determination, never to be wanting or remiss in performing it, but to discharge his simple obligations with the utmost accuracy and diligence.

Again and again, with his mind's eye, he contemplates the beauteous Heaven above, 'the Land of the Living' (Ezech. xxxii. 25), 'the Place of God's Glory' (Isa. lxiii. 15), 'the Everlasting Kingdom' (2 Pet. ii. 4), 'the Promised Land' (Heb. xii. 22), 'the Paradise of God' (Ap. ii. 7), and the 'New Jerusalem' (Ap. xxi. 2), and he knows that within the hallowed walls of that 'City of the Lord of Hosts' (Ps. xlvii. 9) there is gathered every conceivable happiness, and every conceivable delight. What would he not give to be able to throw open the golden gates, and to enter! His heart is stirred to its uttermost depths. He knows that he was created on purpose to enjoy and possess God for all eternity. He feels the attraction; every fibre of his being vibrates with impatience to be with God. His whole nature is strongly drawn towards Him. He hears the Divine words: 'Sponsabo te in sempiternum' (Osee ii. 19), and his whole soul thrills with delight. He understands there *is* no rest and that there *can* be no rest until he can be united with God, and pass within the 'Sanctuary of the Lord' (Deut. xxvi. 15). But how is this to be accomplished? Where will he find the golden key with which he may open the gates of Paradise? He soon learns that the golden key hangs well within the reach of his hands, and that he has only to desire it in order to make it his own. What is that key? It is Sanctity; it is Freedom from sin; it is Innocence of life. This key will open every lock, though no other will turn in one of its wards. 'He that doth the will of My Father, who is in Heaven, he shall enter into the Kingdom of Heaven' (Matt. vii. 21).

So soon as Heaven becomes a reality to us, so soon as we live with this glorious vision ever before our eyes, our present life becomes invested with a new interest; we feel that we are actually building up our future abode, that it will be precisely what we make it; that every day we are (*whether consciously or unconsciously*) adding something to its beauty or else diminishing in some degree its splendour and magnificence, and that it is the one supreme and important reality to be secured at any price, and to be struggled for with unending perseverance. *It is all the more important* to realize all this, because we may, otherwise, soon grow cold and lethargic, and even forfeit our right to eternal life altogether; for, though 'many are called, yet few are chosen.' There is no doubt whatsoever but that God wishes all men to be saved. This momentous and consoling truth is clearly enunciated, in many passages, both in the Old and the New Testament. Thus, to quote a single text from each, Ezechiel writes: 'As I live, saith the Lord, I desire not the death of the wicked, but that the wicked turn away from his evil way and live' (xxxiii. 11). And what Ezechiel says, under he Old Dispensation, St. Peter says, under the

New, in almost identical terms: 'God willeth not that any one should perish, but that ALL should return to penance' (2 Pet. iii. 9).

And, furthermore, as an earnest of the sincerity of His will that all should be saved, He has made the conditions of salvation exceedingly light in themselves, and placed them fully within the easy reach of Catholics. Yet, strange to say, in spite of this, the general opinion seems to be that the majority of *adult* Catholics are lost! Fra E. da Chitignano, O.S.F., in his book, entitled 'L'Uomo in Paradiso' (p. 269), writes: 'St. Jerome, St. Augustine, St. Basil, St. John Chrysostom, St. Ephrem, St. Gregory the Great, and St. Anselm, and many more most learned men, of the highest virtue, have held the opinion that the majority of adult Catholics are condemned to hell for all eternity.' He also says that, 'Even Suarez, who expresses the opposite opinion (*il quale è di contrario parere*), confesses that the more common opinion is against him.'*

* 'Among theologians,' says Father Faber, 'the rigorous opinion regarding the mass of the human race (including infidels and heretics) has crushing authority.

The opinion of such Saints and learned Doctors of the Church is worthy of respect, and deserves to be remembered, and it would be quite out of place for me to express any view in conflict with theirs. But this much I will venture to say, viz., that, as a result of over fifty years of reading, writing, reflecting and experience, I feel I may lay down the following two propositions, *as undoubtedly true:* (1) It is easy for any Catholic to be saved who is really in earnest; (2) And it is easy and very easy for any Catholic to be lost who is not in earnest—who is careless and indifferent. It is not wise to be too sure about our own salvation. The very sense of insecurity is by no means a bad thing. It ensures caution and watchfulness, and will compel us to avoid, as far as possible, the dangerous occasions of sin. 'He that think-

---

The rigorous opinions concerning the damnation of the majority of adult Catholics have more theologians on their side than the milder view! Others maintain that the majority of Catholics will be saved, but that this majority is to be reached only by reckoning all the children and babes.' So careless Catholics must be in much danger! (Consult 'The Creator and the Creature,' by Father Faber, book iii., chap. ii.)

eth himself to stand, let *him* take heed, lest he fall' (1 Cor. x. 12). Consequently, it is just as well to take into account and to allow some weight to the more alarming, yet deliberate, view of the great Saints and Doctors quoted above. For it will set any prudent man thinking and pondering over the best means of rendering his salvation more and more secure, although, personally, I cling to the more hopeful and consoling opinion of the great Suarez.

### I.—VENIAL SIN.

Let us consider a few of these means, as laid down by spiritual writers and teachers. In the first place, we should conceive the most lively appreciation of the inexpressible malice of sin, especially of venial sin. Not, of course, that venial sin can be compared to mortal sin in malice, but merely on the principle that, if we are ever at pains to avoid what is venial, we shall certainly avoid what is mortal. It is really an application of the business principle: 'Look after the pence, and the pounds will look after themselves.' Hate venial sin with all the power of your will, and you will hate mortal sin with still greater intensity, and will never allow it to approach. Guard yourself from the lesser faults, and the more grievous will never be committed. So far as mortal sin is concerned, we are advised to enter upon a serious and detailed consideration of the various consequences that follow from its commission: to weigh them well, and one *at a time.*

Thus, for instance, on Monday we might meditate on the supreme excellence of sanctifying grace, of which it deprives us.

On Tuesday, on the immense value and the inestimable worth of the treasures of merit, accumulated perhaps for many years, of which it robs us, in an instant.

On Wednesday, on the transcendent glory and happiness of Heaven, of which it despoils us.

On Thursday, on the raging fires of hell, which will never end, to which it exposes us.

On Friday, on the most atrocious agony and death of Jesus Christ, which sin, in some sense, renews, according to the words of St. Paul: '*They crucify again to themselves the Son of God, and make Him a mockery'* (Heb. vi. 6).

On Saturday, on the hideousness of sin considered in itself; and

On Sunday, on the black ingratitude and mean selfishness that it involves.

The idea is that we should first of all arouse ourselves to a vivid estimation of *each* of these effects, *taken singly*, and then unite them in one tremendous stream which will overwhelm us, and fill us with the greatest confusion, should we ever find ourselves tampering with temptation, or entering into any negotiation with the fiend.

All spiritual writers, of course, recommend the ordinary means of perseverance, such as the Mass, the Sacraments, Prayer, Meditation, Mortification, the practice of the Presence of God, devotion to the Blessed Virgin Mary, the avoiding of all occasions of sin, and the rest; so there is *no need to dwell upon any of these points*, save in so far as they are treated in some special way. But it may be well to bring to the notice of the benignant reader a few suggestions which are not quite so commonly found in the ordinary treatises.

### II.—PAINS OF PURGATORY.

The first has to do with the doctrine of temporal punishment, endured by the souls in Purgatory. Fra E. da Chitignano lays great stress upon the immense advantages of earnestly considering these sufferings, as nothing will so impress upon us the malice of even venial sin, and the necessity of avoiding the slightest deliberate imperfections. In all these cases, the important thing is to *realize* the dreadful nature of the punishment, and to bring home to ourselves as vividly as possible their agonizing intensity. For with most of us the flames of Purgatory are little more than painted flames, and hardly move us at all. Fra da Chitignano is careful to point out that, as a matter of fact, the sufferings of that dreadful prison are worse than anything of which we have any experience in this life, and that (as St. Thomas himself teaches*) the fire which burns and purifies the holy souls is one and the same

* 'Idem est ignis qui damnatos cruciat in inferno, et qui justos in Purgatorio purgat' (In 4, dist. 20, a. I ad 2, 9).

as that which torments the damned, in the bottomless pit of hell. He quotes St. Catherine of Genoa as declaring that the souls in Purgatory suffer torments that no tongue can describe, and that no mind can understand, unless God should be pleased to enlighten it by a special grace. He then quotes St. M. Maddalena dei Pazzi, who, in her raptures, beheld such terrible and such horrible tortures in Purgatory, 'that all the most horrible torments imagined by Dante, and described by him in his *Divina Commedia,* no more resemble those actually existing in Purgatory than a painted fire resembles a real fire' ('Sono come il fuoco dipinto paragonato al vero,' p. 298).

He also puts considerable emphasis upon the enormous length of time that imperfect souls may have to spend amid the expiatorial fires, which may extend to 'millions and millions of centuries.' That Purgatory exists, and that it is a place of temporal suffering, is, of course, of Divine Faith; but all details as to the degree and as to the length of these sufferings are a matter of opinion and of greater or less probability. What canonized

Saints have declared they have seen, in vision, must certainly be listened to with respect, and should be taken into account in our meditations, but we should also remember that they do not speak with the infallible voice of the Church, and that they neither possess nor claim her Divine authority.

### III.—HELP ALL THOSE WHO ARE IN THEIR LAST AGONY.

Another most efficacious means of securing a holy and a happy death for ourselves is to help others in their last agony, and to obtain for them, by our earnest prayers, the grace of true contrition. It has been calculated by learned statisticians that, every year, 50,000,000 human beings pass before the great judgment seat of God. They tell us that there are at least 150,000 deaths each day; 6,000 each hour; and 100 each minute—that is to say, *considerably more than one every second.* Out of this immense multitude there must be very many but indifferently disposed, and many even altogether unfit to receive a merciful sentence. In innumerable cases nothing but an extraordinary grace can ensure their salvation. How is this grace to be obtained? The apostle St. James tells us, when he says: 'Pray one for another, *that you may be saved.* For, the continual prayer of a just man availeth much' (James v. 16).

If we pray fervently and often for the dying, there can be no doubt but that we shall obtain the grace of true repentance for a considerable number of them, from the most pitiful and compassionate heart of our Divine Lord. We shall obtain the salvation of many who would otherwise have been eternally lost. But observe, at the same time, we shall secure their most devoted friendship for all eternity. It is impossible to conceive the intense gratitude and thankfulness of a soul who finds himself in Heaven, and who realizes that, but for the loving prayers of another, he would now be amid the eternal torments of hell. His whole soul will be filled with the deepest gratitude. He will at once look upon his benefactor as the greatest of his friends. He will ever have his spiritual interests most closely at heart, and will not spare himself any effort until he can, in return, secure for him also the grace of a happy death, and a glorious entry into the heavenly courts.

I would strongly advise my readers to join the 'Pious Union of St. Joseph's Death,' which has its centre at Rome, and which has not only been highly approved by the Sovereign Pontiff, but which has also been enriched by many indulgences. Each member undertakes to pray for the dying, and, if he be a priest, to say a Mass for the same intention, once a year, on a fixed date. Such charity, shown to others, will secure for us many graces from Almighty God, according to the promise: 'Give, and it shall be given to you. . . . For, with the *same measure* that you shall mete, it shall be measured to you again' (Luke vi. 38). Indeed, it is to our own interest to be merciful, for such receive a special blessing from God: 'Blessed are the merciful, since they shall obtain mercy.' Anyone interested should get an admirable little book, from Browne and Nolan, Dublin, written by 'A Marist Father,' entitled 'On the Verge of Eternity, or the Apostolate of Prayer for the Agonizing of Each Day.' We strongly recommend it.

IV.—HELP THE SUFFERING SOULS.

Another very efficacious means of securing a happy eternity is to cultivate a great devotion to the holy souls in Purgatory. By our earnest prayers and Communions and alms and by acts of penance offered up on their behalf, we make for ourselves innumerable friends amongst them. Those who have been helped will never forget their benefactors. If we are able to release a number from their fiery prison, and to obtain for them a speedy entrance into Heaven, we may rest assured that their gratitude will know no bounds. They will take us under their protection, and never cease praying for us until we, too, come to join their ranks. They may, of course, intercede for us while they are still detained amid the cleansing flames; but they will do so with immensely greater power after they have been admitted to the Beatific Vision, and this longed-for moment may be very much hastened by our earnest suffrages. St. Leonard of Port Maurice, during his forty-four years of impressive preaching, was often heard to make use of the following argument:

'Listen to me, my beloved brethren: if you wish to enjoy the delights of Paradise, do all you can to help the souls in Purgatory. For you may be quite sure that if you succeed in rescuing even but one soul, Paradise is yours. Yes! Yes! Paradise is yours. Why? Well, because that holy soul whom you have released will never cease interceding for you, until you join it in Heaven. Do you ask why these souls are so grateful, whereas men in this world are so ungrateful? I will explain. Should you confer a benefit upon a man here, you do but whet his appetite, and dispose him to demand further benefits in the future. Why is this? Because any benefit you may confer upon him is but a partial benefit, and cannot satisfy all his wants. There is nothing final about it. But the benefit you confer upon a soul in Purgatory, when you open the gates of Heaven to him, is final and exhaustive, and completely satisfies all his desires for evermore. He will never ask another benefit. He has every want completely satisfied and every desire gratified. And, as ingratitude is a fault, and quite unknown in Heaven, his one effort will be to obtain for his benefactor a share in his own celestial bliss. He will never fail to intercede for you, and will obtain for you the crowning grace of a death " blessed in the sight of God." '

This seems to be a valuable suggestion, and it may be well worth our while to act upon the advice of the Saint, and to endeavour to do more in the future than we have done in the past for our suffering brethren. In that way we shall secure the valuable help of a host of friends before the throne of God, and obtain a speedy entrance into Heaven.

### V.—INDULGENCES.

Another excellent practice, strongly recommended, is that of gaining as many indulgences as possible. Even apart from its direct effect, such a practice exercises an excellent indirect influence upon the soul. It keeps the thought of the punishment of sin before us; and the severe punishment of even venial sin impresses our minds with a deep sense of its great malice and strengthens our will to resist it; while at the same time we are satisfying for sins, the guilt of which has been forgiven, and getting into the way of making ejaculatory prayers, which should be practised by all who aspire after perfection. This brings us to the sixth suggestion—viz.:

### VI.—EJACULATORY PRAYERS.

One of the simplest and yet one of the most effective means of sanctifying one's soul, and securing a high place in the Kingdom of Heaven, is the habit of uttering ejaculatory prayers. They are short, they can be said at any time, and in any place; they do not interrupt any occupation on which we may be engaged, and at the same time they keep the mind occupied with God and Divine things, and help us to remain habitually sensible of the presence of God. 'The Fathers attach great importance to these frequent, short aspirations towards God, as being well suited to form the spirit of prayer. Cassian, in his *Institutions,* says that it is better to make short prayers, and to *repeat* them more frequently. By multiplying these prayers we unite ourselves more intimately to God, and by making them short, we better escape the darts which the devil hurls against us.'*

The venerable Abbot Blosius, an acknowledged authority on such matters, speaks in even stronger terms. He writes: 'The diligent darting forth of aspirations and prayers of ejaculation and fervent desires to God, joined with true mortification and self-denial, is the *most certain* as well as the shortest way by which a soul can *easily and quickly come to perfection*. And the reason is that aspirations of this kind efficaciously penetrate and surmount all things which are between God and the soul.'†

Cardinal Vives speaks with almost equal fervour in the same sense.‡

* *Vide* 'The Spiritual Life and Prayer,' p. 99.

† *Vide* 'A Book of Spiritual Instruction,' by Blosius, p. 38, chap. v.

‡ Cardinal Vives, O. M. Cap., in his 'Compendium Theol. Ascetico-Mysticae,' p. 259, has the following: 'Jam actum est passim de jaculatoriis orationibus quae quidem interius exteriusque fieri possunt. Sed *nunquam satis adhortari possumus omnes devotos ad illas adhibendas quam frequentissime*, praesertim internas quae faciliores in variis circumstantiis evadunt. Dicito ergo frequenter saltem corde: *Diligam Te Jesu! Fiat voluntas Tua! Coelum! Coelum! O Jesu, quando satiabor in Patria!*—et alia similia.'

This was certainly the opinion of the saintly Father William Doyle, S.J., the well-known army chaplain, whose 'Life' was published in 1920. His biographer tells us that 'it was especially by momentary recollection and ejaculatory prayer that Father Doyle sought to sanctify the passing moment, and to condense perfection into the immediate present. When he was tempted to break a resolution, or when he shrank from some sacrifice, he used to say five times to himself: "Will you refuse to do this for the love of Jesus?" By means of aspirations he sharpened his will into instant action, and brought into play all the accumulated motive-power of the past. . . . He had a wonderful idea of the value of aspirations as a source of grace and merit. "If I knew I should receive one pound sterling for each one I made, I would not waste a spare moment. And yet I get infinitely more than this, though I often fail to realize it." The following are among some of the most beautiful of his favourite aspirations: "My Crucified Jesus, help me to crucify myself. Lord, teach me how to pray, and to pray always." "Jesus,

Thou Saint of saints, make me a saint." "My God, Thou art omnipotent, make me a saint."'* 'The number of aspirations which he contrived to fit into one day, advanced from 10,000 to over 100,000,' says Alfred O'Rahilly, 'though how he was able to make so many remains somewhat of a mystery, for even at the rate of fifty aspirations a minute, it would take over thirty-three hours to make 100,000 ejaculations!'†

If we are intent on fitting ourselves for a place in God's heavenly Kingdom, we shall certainly enter upon this practice of ejaculatory prayers. Besides being a powerful means of advancing, it is so simple and so easy that it is within the reach of everybody. I will merely observe that in selecting our ejaculations, we shall be wise if we are careful to choose (*a*) such aspirations as demand some very specially useful grace, and (*b*) such as are also heavily indulgenced. The following strikes me as fulfilling in a high degree both qualifications—viz., *Sweetest Heart of Jesus, I implore that I may love Thee ever more and more.*

* *Vide* 'Life,' p. 113.

† 'Life,' p. 116, by A. O'Rahilly.

Here, in the first place, we ask for an *increase of the love of God,* which is of greater spiritual advantage to us than anything else for which we could possibly ask. For to increase in God's love is to increase in sanctity, love being the very measure of all holiness both in men and in Angels. In the second place, this aspiration carries with it an *indulgence of three hundred days.* If God cannot refuse the earnest and fervent and continual prayer of the just man, think of the effect of this short prayer repeated many thousand times a day. Then reflect also on the continual multiplication of the three hundred days of indulgence, day by day, as the prayer is repeated over and over again, for hundreds and thousands of times, and on all sorts of occasions, as when dressing and undressing, when lying awake during the night, when travelling or taking a stroll, or while waiting for penitents, in the confessional, or reading or writing, or conversing with others, for such occupations may always be interrupted, just for an imperceptible moment, to cast a loving glimpse at God, present within us, and to ask Him for a further increase of love.

### VII.—COMPLIN.

Since a happy death is an essential condition of a happy eternity, and as no one can promise himself so great a grace, or know with absolute certainty that it will be given him, unless indeed he receive a Divine revelation on the subject, it becomes exceedingly necessary to make it a subject of regular and persevering prayer. There can be no doubt whatever but that God will grant us any gift needed to ensure our salvation, if only we ask for it earnestly and to the end. To pray for it daily is, no doubt, to secure it without fail. 'Ask, and you shall receive.'

Now, there is no better method of persevering in our prayers for a happy death than by connecting them in some way with our daily recitation of the Breviary. Complin may be offered up, in an especial way, every day of our lives, for this end. Whenever we say: 'Noctem quietam et finem perfectum concedat nobis Dominus omnipotens' (May the Almighty Lord grant us a quiet night and a perfect end), we naturally think of our death. For, what is this 'night' but the

close of the short ' day ' of our present life ? What is this *night* but the night spoken of by Our Lord, when He said, *The night cometh when no man can work* (John ix. 4). Hence, we pray that this night of death may be ' quiet '—that is to say, peaceful, and free from the anguish of remorse, and from the violent assaults and temptations of the devil. ' *Et finem perfectum* ' (And the end perfect). The end, that is to say, the final act of our conscious life; the going forth from this world, may it be perfect, that is to say, accompanied with all the usual formalities of Viaticum, Extreme Unction, the Last Blessing, and the rest. Such should be the thoughts in our minds, as we recite the familiar words: ' Noctem quietam et finem perfectum concedat nobis Dominus omnipotens. Amen.'

Such a petition, offered up to God, day after day, as we recite our Office, is certain to secure for us all that is requisite in our last hour. A prayer such as this, repeated and repeated with the regularity of the town clock, and persevered in even to our old age, becomes irresistible, and is quite sure of obtaining grace and mercy and a peaceful and perfect

end, when, at last, the Angel of Death is sent to summon us before the Great White Throne, to listen to the solemn sentence which is to determine our fate for evermore. 'O! Quando veniam, et apparebo ante faciem Tuam? Quando satiabor gloria Tua? Quando totus et totaliter amabo Te, et Te solo fruar?'

CPSIA information can be obtained
at www.ICGtesting.com
Printed in the USA
LVHW052013210921
698368LV00008B/532